MURKEY'S

Email us at: ldc@loucook.com

For more about Bunzini, Webster and the Guys: bunzini.com

© 2017 Lou Cook
ISBN 978-1-7335428-1-4
BRAP! Productions, Publisher

Dedication

Dedicated to the Rabbit.
Of course.

And in fond Memory of:

Chuck
Jim N.
Short Pants
Craiggers
and especially Rocky

MURKEY'S

A RABBIT NOIR

By LOU COOK

Illustrations:
E.A. SAWABINI
Photographs:
LOU COOK

Contents

The Players

In Order of Appearance:

Bunz, the Rabbit: former Pie Inspector for the city, loves Murkey's, especially the pies

Ida, hard-working rabbit: late-night waitress at Murkey's, afternoon barkeep at The Anchor

Webbs, the Spider: Bunz's special pal, loves Murkey's, especially the donuts

Hamms, the hamster: head baker at Murkey's

Bongo, the dog: an affable dog

Captain G.G.: a dog down on her luck, captain of the fishboat *Sea Dog*

Moose M'Boy: ex-sugar smuggler, recently released from 10 years in the Moosegow

Smilin' Moose: sidekick of Moose M'Boy, also recently released from the Moosegow

Doc, the tiger: late-night cook at Murkey's, resident of Sipp's Creek

Joe Martuuni and his Pops: two pelicans, owners of the fishboat *Fishy Lady*

Nosey Parker: a seagull, always on the lookout for intel and food

Bill the Bum, another moose: owns a houseboat on Sipp's Creek, resident on the wrong side of the law

Juke and Jake: two guard gulls for the Sipp's Creek residents

Marilyn the Librarian, another spider: loves books and a good adventure

1: Looking for the Spider

See that cuppa coffee and donut? That little drawing was sketched on a napkin in Murkey's Diner one night, and it's got me thinking of a story. Does that ever happen to you? It could be a doodle on a napkin, a postcard from that cold beach weekend in December, or the little plastic tray with the photo of San Remo that holds memories of the summer you traveled Italy by yourself. Now and then, you take a look and remember.

Now this story, it's about Murkey's Diner. Open 24 Hours. It's been on Pier 13 forever. From the outside, maybe it's no beauty. The inside secret is this: Murkey's has the best coffee and pastry in town. It's been a friendly harbor for travel-weary seamen, local stevedores and long-haul truckers passing through town. It has the terrific coffee that every cabbie and night watchman count on. And if you're in the know, you go there too.

Yet and still, here's a curious fact: nobody

knows for sure how the place got started. History has blurred, but here's what I've heard: the original place was a walk-up lunch counter, owned by Murkey and Sprinkhels.

Those two just couldn't get along. They would fight and argue all up and down The Embarcadero waterfront. They put on quite a show, and everybody swarming the waterfront back then, scuffling to make a buck, would take a break and watch them brawl.

A certain day came and Murkey didn't turn up. No one saw or heard from him again. The waterfront could be hazardous, and Guys wondered: had Murkey left town? Been killed? Shanghaied? Did Sprinkhels care? No. He took over the lunch counter, never said a word, and never changed the name.

Here's another story though: there was this dubious jockey and local tout, name of "Turf" Murkey. Some say he started up the lunch counter after he was banned permanent from horseracing. Maybe behind the lunch counter was a little room where he ran a certain private gambling den. At least he ran it until he lost it all in poker to Old Man Sprinkhels.

One way or another, Sprinkhels ended up with the place, and the Sprinkhels family has owned Murkey's continuous for three generations. When alcohol was banned, a lunch counter on the wharf was the perfect spot for boats to sneak in illegal Canadian whiskey. Sprinkhels grasped the opportunity. During that first Prohibition, he made so much money, he invested in a sugar plantation.

By the time Prohibition was repealed, he had a sugar empire. He got so rich, he became respectable. He made lots of friends at City Hall. He built a museum and rebuilt his little lunch counter into a real diner.

So now, to our story. About ten years ago, our fine state inflicted another prohibition on society by outlawing sugar—at least they tried to. To try and stop the sugar smuggling, a whole new category of government inspector was set up. They were a tough bunch that got named the Pie Inspector Team—the P.I.T.s.

During this Sugar Ban, smuggling sugar got huge! Piles of money changed hands. Wouldn't you figure that, once again, the diner was the perfect location for smuggling? Sprinkhels Junior, grandson of the sugar baron, moved sugar around the way his grandfather had moved booze.

Of course, I'm not saying this is the verified truth. Junior never got caught. But spend time in the right places and you will hear all kinds of stories. Some are bound to be true.

Through all these years, Murkey's remains the best diner in town. But the city? It keeps changing. A new scuffling crowd has flooded in, fighting for their chunk of change. These days the big money is in real estate. Real estate prices have levitated out of sight. The good ol' places—Crab's Corner, Sam's Whoopie, The Old Spike—all closed down. They plain couldn't afford to do business any more.

And a new rumor about Murkey's is going around. It's said that Murkey's little spot on the waterfront caught someone's mercenary eye. Late one night, a rabbit named Bunz heard that rumor.

The stocky, long-eared rabbit sat on his usual stool in the diner, sipping coffee and waiting for his spider pal, Webbs. Webbs was late. The clock ticked. Bunz spun around on his stool while Ida cleared tables.

Where could that spider be?

Abruptly, Bunz stood up. "Hey, Ida. If that crazy spider shows up, tell him I'll be back."

"Will do, Bunz."

The glass door swung shut behind him. Bunz looked up and down the empty Embarcadero. No traffic. No spider. A thick fog. The shadows cast by the streetlights snaked across his memories of the crooks and sorry deviants who used to prowl the docks at night. He was on the docks with them, his Pie Inspector Team on the chase. The full-time sugar smugglers doing the big business, and the little chiselers who sold half-cup baggies for forty-fifty bucks, intent on their illegal errands.

But not tonight. Not anymore. The Sugar Ban was over, the Pie Inspectors decommissioned. The waterfront was dead. The fog pressed against the streetlights and dripped from the roofs of old pier sheds. It was so wet, it was almost rain.

Bunz hunched into his trench coat and wondered, *What are all those jokers up to now?* The thought passed and he considered the present question. Where was Webbs? He was not at Murkey's as he was supposed to be. If a cruise ship was in port, he might be at Pier 27, talking to longshore Guys. Webbs loved to collect waterfront stories, and those longshore Guys told amazing stories from the days when the waterfront was booming and the city was the center of West Coast shipping.

Might as well check there.

The rabbit turned north along The Embarcadero. The streetcar tracks ran down the middle of the roadway on his left, and the dark, veiled bay was to his right. As he walked along, he rattled doorknobs and poked his head into a pier shed or two. No night watchmen had seen the spider that night.

Ahead he saw Pier 27. No fancy cruise ship loomed above the pier shed, although a longshore Guy told Bunz that a ship was due to dock before dawn. But no, he had not seen Webbs. Bunz walked further north, past the darkened souvenir shops to the commercial fish docks. He could hear the foghorn sounding at the Golden Gate, warning ship traffic of the narrow passage through the headlands. Still, there was no spider.

The rabbit turned and retraced his route. At Murkey's, he glanced inside the misted window. Empty. *Might as well keep going south,* he decided. *Don't feel like sitting around.*

As Bunz neared the Ferry Building, a hazy light beam caught his eye from across The Embarcadero. He stopped and looked. A narrow shred of light illuminated the stoop of an unkempt Victorian house. That building had been abandoned for years. Why was the light on?

He stepped across the empty lanes of The Embarcadero and the streetcar tracks, his eye focused on the stoop. From the open front door, dim light shone on a vague but familiar silhouette.

He climbed the chipped terrazzo steps. The fur on the back of his neck prickled. The shape highlighted on the stoop looked familiar because it was Webbs' straw hat! Bunz leaned down and picked it up. It was damp with fog, so it had been there awhile. He looked up at the empty old pile. Despite light shining through the open door, the place appeared empty, its windows dark. Unwelcome possibilities ran through his mind.

Get a grip, B, he thought. *This isn't the old waterfront. There's a light on, the door is open. Webbs' hat is on the stoop. You don't know why. Go in. Check it out.*

He nudged the front door further open and peered in. A dank smell reeking of unrepaired roofs and bad plumbing wafted out. One low-watt lightbulb in a three-armed wall sconce barely lit the entry hall. Loose wires poked through a hole in the clammy plaster. A stairwell squeezed into the narrow hall, stopping a few stingy feet short of the threshold. At the far end of the hall, a door frame barely held a door sagging on one hinge. In the shadowy silence, Bunz heard a voice, too faint to understand, coming from the rear doorway.

He stepped through the street door and eased down the hall. A floorboard creaked. He winced and slowed his pace. At the sagging door, he stopped, cocked a long ear, and waited to hear the voice again.

"I'm out," the voice said. Bunz tipped his head. It sounded familiar. He couldn't quite place it.

A second voice said, "Hamms?"

Hah! A voice he knew as well as his own.

Webbs' voice! He relaxed. *That crazy spider,* he thought. *Playing cards? Here?*

"Hit me," said a third voice.

Bunz slid carefully onto the wooden step leading one flight down. He set his weight gently, but the worn steps creaked. Three steps from the bottom, he paused to watch. Nobody looked over. The three Guys were focused on their card game.

Bunz sees the card game.

Bunz waved the damp straw hat in the air. "Somebody lose a hat?"

Webbs turned from his cards, his round orange nose quivering with surprise.

"Bunz! My hat!"

Hamms glanced briefly in Bunz's direction and then scowled at his cards.

"Oh, this old thing?" Bunz said, twirling it above his head as he headed toward the card table. "I picked up this hat on the street." He put it on his own head. "Abandoned, don't you know. What do you think?" he asked, setting it at a jaunty angle on top of his hat. "Is it me?"

"No, Bunz." The spider returned to his cards. "I forgot it on the stoop, didn't I?" Webbs shook his head and laid his cards face down. "When Bongo didn't answer the door, I climbed up to a second-story window."

Hamms checked his watch. "Oops. Gotta fold, Guys. I'm due at Murkey's."

"Somebody else was due at Murkey's," said Bunz, giving his pal a penetrating look.

Webbs ignored this and concentrated on gathering the cards. "Hamms and I came over to keep Bongo company here at his new job."

Bunz turned to Bongo. "What? You're watchdog at this dump? What's here to watch?"

"It's a job." The dog pushed his cards toward Webbs. "The place has finally been sold. They're gonna fix it up."

"Well, I found the front door open, watchdog."

Bongo looked across at the hamster. "Left it

open for you, Hamms. You were late."

"Yeah. It sticks maybe, and doesn't close all the way." Hamms stood up. "But tell me, who's going to break in here?"

Bunz frowned at Hamms, "Squatters."

Hamms moved toward the stairs. "What squatters," he said, and looked around. "Did I miss squatters somewhere?"

"Looks like we played longer than I realized," said Webbs as he set the cards in the middle of the table.

"You think?" said Bunz.

Webbs smiled to himself and changed the subject. "B., you'll never guess what Hamms told me."

"What?"

"Word is, someone's been asking around about Murkey's."

"WHAT!" Bunz said. "Asking what?"

"Don't know. We're wondering, too. Maybe it's going to get bought out. Like everything else these days," said Webbs.

"You can't mess with Murkey's! Best coffee and pie in town!" Bunz said. The others nodded. "Who is it, asking around?"

"That's the thing. Nobody knows. Strangers. Hamms heard about it at the diner. Tell him, Hamms."

"Yeah, yeah, but on the way. Let's get going."

Webbs followed the hamster up the creaky stairs. A few steps up, he reached over the stair rail, lifted his hat off Bunz's head and settled it on his own. Behind him, Bongo turned off the light and carefully felt his way up the stairs.

They trooped out into the fog. Bongo heaved the door shut and turned an old iron key to lock the empty building.

"No relief guard? You're leaving all this to fate?" asked Bunz, gesturing at the dark old building.

"That relief Guy—he's always late." Bongo stepped past Bunz and peered down the street. "He'll be here soon enough." The little dog propped the door key into a corner shadow.

Bunz said nothing and hustled after the hamster's speedy little legs. "So, Hamms. What's this about Murkey's?"

"All I know is this. Ida was working her other job at the Old Anchor. Two moose come in to the bar. Asked stuff about Murkey's. Ida said their questions sounded like they were fishing for real estate information. You know how crazy real estate is these days."

They knew what he meant. These days everything was up for sale.

"Two moose? Anyone know them? Seen them?" Bunz asked.

They shook their heads no.

So.

Nobody knows. Mystery moose asking questions about their favorite diner? Did someone have plans to take it over? What was going on?

You might rightly say our story started not this foggy night, but ten years back. And just yesterday the second chapter began.

2: 12 Hours Earlier

G.G., a big white dog with floppy ears, stood on the deck of the *Sea Dog* and directed her hose at the bird poop splattered all over her boat, every day. She aimed at the hull of her little skiff, the *Pup*, stowed upside-down on the roof of the wheelhouse. More poop. *Those so-and-so racketeering seagulls,* she groused. *Wish I could afford to pay them off.* But she couldn't. Money was tight. She was lucky to afford her berth fees. She watched the poopy water drain off the boat. Her tail drooped.

"Hey, you! Wit da hose!"

G.G. turned her head and looked toward the wharf where a big moose and a short moose stood side-by-side, watching her. The big one was almost as big as G.G.

"We want ta go out fer a couple hours ta-night," the big one growled. "How much?"

For sure he looks like trouble, she thought.

And the short one—he had a smile that was too smiley. She felt a chill. She knew that smiley smile. And it *was* trouble. The last time she'd heard about that smile, it was headed for the Moosegow with a five-to-ten-year sentence.

G.G. meets the two moose.

Now here it was, back in her face.

Maybe I just turn the hose on 'em, she thought. *And good riddance.*

Excellent idea, except for one thing: trouble. As in money trouble: unpaid electric bill; a bilge pump that needed parts; seagull poop all over. In fact, trouble all over. And now these two.

Her grump slipped down a couple more

notches. No way around it, she needed work. Bad. She leaned down and slowly turned off the hose, then turned and looked back at the moose. If they had cash money, she wouldn't turn it down. But it had to be cash.

"So, who's asking?" G.G. said.

"Waddya ya think? I am!" the big one said.

The smiley one just stood there, eyeing her. She eyed him back and snapped, "What are you looking at?"

His smile widened. "Looking at you, Big Dog. Remember me?"

She ignored the question. "It'll have to be cash. Cash money only."

"Jus' tell me how much it is first, Smart Dog," said the big one. "One, two hours maybe. What's th' freight?"

"You just going for a ride? You want to fish? Got somewhere to go?" she asked, thinking about how much to charge these jokers.

"Jus' wanta ride around, along the waterfront. Relive old memories." The big moose laughed unpleasantly. The little one snorted.

Yeah, right. Just the type for that. Maybe if I charge too much, they'll turn me down.

"Just for you two romantics, and we stay in the bay, $300 per hour plus fuel."

"Plus fuel? Highway robbery an' contortion!" The big moose scowled. "But cheaper than dose other crooks. I'll pay ya $285, cash money. No extra fer fuel. How's by that?"

She studied the big moose. If the other fishermen had asked more than that, obviously none of them wanted anything to do with these two. Maybe they could afford to be choosey. G.G. could not. She let the pause lengthen, to make it seem like she was reluctant. Heck, she was reluctant. Her boat swayed beneath her feet, reminding her she needed their money.

"Make it $285 per hour or any part of an hour, and I guess I'll do it. Money up front. $285 now, the rest when we see how long we're out. And we stay in the bay."

Just for that smilin' clown you're with, I should charge you double.

"Yeah, yeah." Moose M'Boy peeled money from a stack of bills and handed it to his pint-size sidekick. The smiley smile widened. Leaning over, with a wink he handed the cash to G.G. Ignoring him, she counted out the money.

"When we goin' out, Moose?" the short moose asked.

"Shaddup like I told ya!" Moose growled.

"Yeah, what time?" G.G. asked. These checkered clowns were bugging her. She shoved the bills deep into a pocket. But this was cash money and more from where this came. If they walked away and didn't come back, that would be OK. The big dog now had $285.

Moose said, "Make sure yer here nine tanight. We got stuff ta do. We get here when we get here."

"OK, then. Clock starts at nine whether you're here or not."

"You jus' make sure you're here when we are!" The two moved off the wharf.

Fingering the money in her pocket, she watched them walk away. "Nothing illegal," she called after them. "And I'm not waiting up all night."

She stood on her deck and felt the *Sea Dog* shift in the pull of the waning tide. Her gaze rested on the stubborn, dried-on poop and she reached for the long-handled scrub brush. If only she could afford the payola to those blankety-blank seagulls, life would be so much sweeter. She shook her head and turned the hose back on. The sun shone bright on the dirty wash-down water as it ran across the deck and out the scuppers.

Let's see. I need to fuel up, fill the water tank, pump out the sewage, and check the running lights. I got time to pick up some food.

Out to sea, just beyond the steep and rocky headlands, a massive fog bank piled up. By late afternoon, grey covered the coast, overtopping the headlands. Invisible above the fog, the full moon pulled at the tide. An extra-high tide was predicted. The low tide turned, and tidal currents swirled in again through the narrow Golden Gate. The fog, playing tag with the inrushing waters, swept in and muffled the bay.

Afternoon fog at the gate.

3: Midnight at the Diner

Late night at Murkey's. Tedious tonight. No ships due in port till morning, so no longshore Guys stopping by for an early coffee. Too late to be out if you worked nine to five. Too early for truckers; too early for fishermen or ferry crews to drop by on their way to work aboard their boats. No cab drivers waiting for that last fare. Slowest part of the night.

And much too slow for Ida. She was a bored rabbit. Her short ears drooped as she picked her teeth and watched the fog condense on the window. Every few seconds, moisture formed a drop and slid down the glass. She listened to the clock tick, tick, tick.

No action. Nada. Zilchville. Nothing remained to prepare for the morning rush. She had left one table to clear, just for something to do, in a minute.

Old Man Sprinkhels peered from his frame in the wall photo.

He prefers it when the place is hopping, she thought. *Just like I do.*

All was quiet, even back in the kitchen.

Earlier, Doc, the late-night cook, had made lots of noise scrubbing pots and pans. Now, there was only silence.

Ida pushed open the swing door to the kitchen and called out, "Need any help back here?"

"What?" came Doc's muffled reply.

Flipping the street door buzzer on, she entered the kitchen. Walking toward the back, she saw Doc. The door to the big, walk-in refrigerator was open, and the husky little tiger was inside.

"What'cha doin', Doc?"

"Aww. Gets so busy during the day, the fridge turns into a durn mess. Can't find a thing without a trained blood hound." He dropped celery stalks into their box.

In her thin polyester uniform, Ida shivered in the cool air. As Doc's fur was thicker than hers, he didn't notice the cold.

"Got something I can do that's not in the fridge? I got a few dishes for the washer, but that's it."

"Why don't you clear out the washer and put the dirty dishes in. And those pots on the drain board are probably dry. Hang 'em by the range."

"I'm on it," she said, and began to make her own noise with the pots and pans.

Walking through the night, making their

way past dark piers, Bunz and the Guys closed in on the diner. Long pier sheds stretched invisibly into the thick bay fog. Out in the deepwater channel, an unseeable ship crept by, sounding two prolonged warning blasts on its foghorn every two minutes.

Small boats, beware! Not a night anyone would choose to be out on the water.

Bunz was no professional sailor, but it was obvious that the tide was extra high. Water lapped at the underside of the piers and threatened to flood The Embarcadero. Tidal currents in the bay were notoriously fast and tricky. Strong currents could turn even a large ship off course and onto the rocks. Or into a bridge tower. It was challenging to locate the navigation buoys and lights that guided ships safely in the dense fog. It was impossible to see the unlighted debris. All manner of junk floated through the bay, seized by the fast currents: tree trunks, tires, trash—all of it a hazard to navigation.

For those on land, an orange neon sign was their beacon in the cold fog: MURKEY'S, OPEN 24 HOURS. It shone through the dark night and reflected off the wet pavement. Along with great coffee and pastry, Murkey's was famous for its crazy neon sign. Approached from the north, the vertical sign read "MURKEY'S." Precise and proper. But viewed from the south, the way the Guys were approaching now, it was kinda goofy. It still read "MURKEY'S," but the letters were flipped. The M, the U and the Y looked normal from either side. But from the south side, the R, the K, the E and the S were flipped backward.

This always tickled Bunz. He smiled to himself as they approached. Seeing the sign meant that soon he would enjoy hot coffee and warm pie.

Ida was hanging up pots when the street door buzzer sounded. She stuck her head around the kitchen door to see who was there. She grinned.

"Hi, Guys! Hey, Bunz! Long time, no see!"

"Hey-hey! Ida! How's it going." They greeted her with wide smiles as they sat down at the counter. Everybody was happy when they arrived at Murkey's.

"I see you found your friend, Inspector," she said to Bunz.

"If I was still an inspector, he'd be sorry I found him," Bunz said, giving Webbs a little fake punch.

She laughed and took a moment to look at the friendly faces.

"OK. Who wants regular coffee, who wants 'spresso?" she asked. She placed a bet with herself: Webbs would order a donut and 'spresso. Bunz, warm pie and coffee. Bongo, you never knew. Hamms never seemed to eat.

"Espresso!" said Webbs.

"Coffee," the others said in chorus.

"OK. Coming right up."

She set out cups and poured coffee. "And we have glazed donuts—"

"That's for me!" said Webbs.

"—cherry pie and banana cream pie, and these new glutton-free muffins that have a pineapple slice on top." She gave a sideways glance at Hamms. "They aren't half bad if you toast 'em. And day-old, we have chocolate-chip maple cookies. Half off."

"Warm pie for me," said Bunz. "Cherry."

"Cookies, please," said Bongo, stirring sugar into his coffee.

"Just coffee," said Hamms.

Doc stuck his head out around the kitchen door and waved a sponge. "Hey, Guys! What's shakin'?" he asked.

"Doc! Hey, Guy! What's happenin' with you? How's business?" They all spoke at once.

"Doing good, good. Just cleaning up and getting ready for deliveries. Duck Trucking should be here soon." He looked at Hamms. As baker and senior employee, Hamms was top chef at Murkey's and darn particular about having his kitchen just so.

"Any special requests, Hamms?" Doc asked.

"No, no," Hamms said. He picked up his

coffee. "I'll be back there in a minute."

Doc disappeared back into the kitchen and the door swung shut behind him.

Bunz said, "Hey, Ida. Hamms said someone's been asking about Murkey's."

"You must mean those types I had at the bar the other day," she said. She set a glistening donut in front of Webbs.

"Two moose?" said Bunz.

She put warm pie, cherries oozing, in front of Bunz and a small plate filled with cookies next to Bongo's coffee.

"Yeah. They were complaining about the lousy breakfast at that pancake joint over by the ferry docks."

She split a pineapple muffin in half, put it in the toaster, and leaned against the counter while it toasted. "That's how Murkey's came up. I told them this was a better place and they should eat here." She sipped her coffee.

Bunz speared a fat cherry. "Did they come here?"

She shrugged. "Don't know."

"Hamms said maybe they were real estate Guys?"

Hamms slid off his stool. No time for talk. Time to see how messed up his kitchen had gotten since yesterday.

"Maybe." Ida took the muffin out of the toaster and watched a pat of butter melt in.

"I see a lot of Guys all day, right? You get hunches. With these two, there was something kinda off, you know? Besides, everyone on the waterfront knows Murkey's. Only a tourist will ask about it, like: where is Murkey's, how is the food, what are the hours." She picked up the muffin.

"So?" Bunz prompted her.

"They wanted to know when did deliveries come? How many Guys work here? When's the shift change? When is it busy? Like that." She bit into the muffin and chewed slowly.

Bunz nodded. "Maybe stuff you'd ask if you wanted to buy the place."

Ida spoke over the deep growl rumbling in Bongo's throat. "That was Joe Maartuni's idea. He was there. He saw them."

Bunz laid his fork down. "Joe's back?"

"Yeah. He's fishing with his Pops again."

Webbs said, "You'd make good money selling Murkey's right now." He saw the indignant looks the others gave him and added, "I mean, you know, the way real estate is."

"B-Jeez, Webbs," Ida said. Her ears drooped. "I hope you're wrong."

Bongo growled again and bit down on a cookie. Ida watched cookie crumbs dance across her clean counter. She resisted the urge to point this out.

"Sprinkhels Junior wouldn't sell, would he?" she asked. "That family's owned this pie palace forever."

"Yeah," said Bunz. "But they didn't get so blinkin' rich by turning down money."

"Yeah," Webbs said sarcastically. "What did Junior do during the last land boom? Sold off their original sugar warehouse in Mission Bay. It's condos now."

"Types like that never have enough money," Bongo groused.

"Tell me, what do these two Guys look like?" Bunz said, returning to the subject at hand.

With her paws Ida measured two contrasting heights. "One short spurt, one big brick."

"Mutt and Jeff," Bunz said to himself. "What else?"

"Well, the short spurt had a beer. The brick, he wanted a moosecatel fizz." She grinned.

Bunz laughed. "Did he get it?"

Ida snorted. "Not at the Old Anchor. He had a gin and ginger."

Bunz pondered. "That pancake place is next to the Lodge Motel. Suppose they're staying there?"

"Well, Joe mentioned he'd seen them up at the fish docks. So maybe they're looking all around the—"

Ida stopped abruptly as the diner jerked

them all with a sharp, hard shake. From the kitchen, pots clanged together.

Everybody's first thought was *"EARTH-QUAKE!"*

"What the *heck*?" said Bongo.

They braced for another shake.

Ida turned and disappeared into the kitchen. Bongo slid off his stool and followed her through the swinging door. She was surprised to see Hamms and Doc at the chef's desk, calmly confering over supplies and making out a purchase list.

"You OK?" Ida asked.

"Some flotsam hit the pier, that's all," Hamms said without looking up.

Doc noticed her anxious face and said, "Moon's full tonight, so the tide's extra high. A lot of junk's floating around the bay."

Just then a bigger THUNK rattled the diner. Ida jumped and reached out a paw to steady herself. The pans clanged, harder this time.

"Must be plenty big," Ida said. She looked at them with worried eyes. "It won't damage the pier?"

Hamms tossed his pencil down and sighed. "Unlikely. But suppose we take a look."

Doc and Ida followed Hamms to an open area in the kitchen. A hatch cover was set into the thick, old floor planking. Bongo watched as the two cooks and Ida leaned over and took hold of a large, iron-ring handle recessed into the three-foot-square hatch. They heaved up.

"Errrffff!"

The hatch cover did not move. Another THUNK shook them all.

Ida asked, "When's the last time this thing was opened up?"

"Years," Hamms grunted. He shot a look at Bongo. "Give a hand here."

Bongo squeezed in and grabbed hold.

They all heaved together. The stiff old hinges resisted.

"Hold on!" Ida trotted over to the range, grabbed the can of cooking oil and snagged a broom leaning against the wall as she came back. She poured some oil on the hinges.

They leaned over the hatch cover again and heaved. Slowly a crack appeared between the floor planks and the hatch cover. Ida shoved the broom handle into the crack, keeping the cover from dropping back down.

Bunz strolled into the kitchen.

"Oh ho!" he said, eyes sparkling. "Opening up the old hatch, eh?"

He took a grip in the widening gap and strained with the rest. The old hinges creaked and groaned.

SCRREEEE-ch!

Slowly they raised the hatch cover all the

way up and swung it backward onto the kitchen floor.

They peer down through the hatch at the waters below.

Everybody leaned over and looked through the opening. The dark and restless bay waters weren't so very far below. As they watched, the end of a huge log, floating vertically in the water, lazily broke the surface. Eighteen inches in diameter, it bobbed up a foot above the water surface and sank down again.

"Wow!" said Doc.

"Look how slowly it moves," Ida said.

"Waterlogged big-time," Doc said. "Been in the water a good long time."

"How deep is the water here, right now?" asked Bunz.

"With the tide high like this, at least fifteen feet. It deepens pretty quick the further out the pier you go."

Ida pushed the handle of the broom hard against the deadhead. It sank beneath the water and casually bobbed up again. "It's so big! I can't believe it worked its way under the pier through all the pilings!" she said.

An invisible current grabbed the piling. It rose up and THUNKED against the edge of the hatchway. The floor shook.

"Happens now and then," said Hamms.

Ida shoved the broom handle down against the deadhead again and gave it a firm push toward the open waters of the bay. Reluctantly it bobbed off into the darkness, caught up by a passing current.

There was one more distant thud, and then all was quiet. The coolness of the bay slunk up into the kitchen.

"OK. Fun's over. Let's close this thing up," ordered Hamms. "Time's a tickin'. I got pies to make."

4: After Coffee

Webbs polished off the last few donut crumbs from his plate and sighed with pleasure.

Geez, I love this place, he thought. Those loud thunks shaking the diner? He'd heard that before. Some flotsam trapped under the pier; it would soon float away. No big deal.

He smiled. *When I was a young spider, first stop after school—Murkey's!*

Back when Rufus Cain was head baker.

He'd slip me a donut, if Gran'dad wasn't looking.

He turned and looked around his home away from home. Same old wooden chairs, same old scratched laminate tabletops, same old chrome stools. From the framed photo by the door, Old Man Sprinkhels gazed down: the Old Man stood proud in front of the iron gates of his first sugar factory, in a black suit and tall hat. Sure, he made his Big Money in the sugar business, but this little diner was where he started.

Gran'dad had maintained that the little

diner on Pier 13 held a warm spot in Old Man Sprinkhels' mercenary heart, and that the Old Man always said the place could never be sold. But did Sprinkhels' grandson, Junior, feel the same way? That was the big question.

Webbs sighed and stared at the stalwart guardian of the old diner. How long would it take to knock the old place down? Five minutes?

"You'd never let them sell this place, would you?" he asked the photo. Webbs would swear he saw the old boy shake his head 'no'.

Just then Bunz pushed through the door from the kitchen. He cocked his head at the spider.

"Who you talking to, Webbs?"

"Oh, no one, no one," the spider replied as he spun his stool around, a bit embarrassed.

"Well," Bunz said, cheerfully retaking his seat, "somewhere an old pier is breaking apart."

"Always. These high tides love finding old junk to play with."

"Oh yeah! You should have seen this piling!"

Webbs stopped spinning and looked at Bunz. "You saw it?"

"Sure did! We opened up that old hatch."

"Really?" Webbs turned to Bunz, eyes wide.

"Yeah, and it took some work," Bunz said,

pleased with his recent effort.

"Gee dang it! I've never seen it open. When I was little, Rufus made it real plain that if I fooled around with it, I'd get no donut." He exchanged a look with Bunz. "I do have my priorities!"

Bunz chuckled. "You do."

"He always said 'Never even think about going under the pier.'"

"Never looked under this pier myself."

"Not even during the Sugar Ban?"

"This end of the waterfront, no. Never my beat. This is where I got my pie. I got priorities, too," Bunz said.

Bongo came out of the kitchen nibbling a piece of bacon.

"So, what about these mooses?" The little dog sat down next to Webbs.

Webbs said, "The plural of moose is moose, Bongo."

"It is? That's stupid. It should be mooses."

"Well, that's what it is."

Bunz said, "Mooses or moose, either way, I'm gonna find 'em." His voice hardened. "Hand 'em some advice."

Bongo growled his assent and asked, "So where do we start?"

"With Joe Maartuni. Find out what he saw at the fish docks." Bunz eyed the clock. "The fish boats will be heading out soon. Let's move." He turned to Webbs and asked his pal, "You coming?"

Webbs frowned, staring absently at the wall. The rabbit waved a paw in front of the spider's face.

"Webbs? You're lost in space, Spide."

The spider turned and focused his eyes on the rabbit. "Well, here's the thing, B. These moose Guys are asking funny questions, I mean 'funny' if they're truly real estate Guys."

Bunz frowned. "And?"

"If they're interested in Murkey's as real estate, it's for the location, not this old building."

Bunz's voice grated. "Your point?"

"So why ask questions about Murkey's operation, if they're going to tear the place down?"

Bunz scowled at the thought. His eyes darkened.

Webbs went on, "I'm just wondering what else they might be up to."

Bunz stood. "Tell you what. When I find 'em, I'll ask 'em di-rectly."

Bongo jumped to his feet, tail wagging, eyes gleaming. Bunz eyed the eager dog. Bongo wasn't the most meticulous tracker, but maybe he would be useful.

"So, you coming?" Bunz asked the spider.

Webbs did not hear the question—he was

chasing a feeling way at the back of his spider mind that floated there, but wouldn't settle into a clear thought.

Bunz shook his head. He knew. If Webbs wasn't ready, you couldn't move him. The rabbit turned to Bongo. "Let's move. I want to catch Joe and his Pops before they leave port." Bongo's tail thumped against his stool. He was ready.

Bunz glanced back at Webbs. "See you here later, then."

"You know, Bunz," Webbs called after the departing duo, "if you see any gulls, have a little chat. Those gulls don't miss much."

The two Guys set a northerly course along The Embarcadero. Twenty minutes later, the smell and sound of diesel generators floated in the air. They had reached the working fish docks. Boats were being readied for a day of fishing. Boat engines came to life with a satisfactory rumble, and one by one, fish boats made their way into the foggy bay waters.

The slips next to the *Fishy Lady* were already empty but the *Fishy Lady* was still tied up. Pops Maartuni was in the wheelhouse. The radio was tuned to Vessel Traffic, and he listened to reports of ship movements in and out of the bay as he checked gauges and adjusted the radar screen. Joe Maartuni was on deck, stowing the stores: bait for the fish, food and coffee for him and his Pops. A few boxes were still stacked on the wharf, waiting to be stowed on the boat.

"Hey, Joe," B. called out. "Need some help there?"

The young pelican peered up from the deck of the *Fishy Lady* to see who else was awake this early.

"Bunz! Bongo, hi!" said Joe. "Yeah, toss that stuff on down."

From the wheelhouse door, Pops Maartuni waved a wing at them. The Guys waved back and began to hand boxes down to the younger pelican.

"Thanks, Guys! But, hey! What brings you down here at o-dark-thirty?" Joe asked.

"Those two moose that were at the Old Anchor. Ida says you saw them up this way."

"Oh. Those two." Joe nodded. "Yeah. Coupla strange ones."

"Any particular reason you say that?" Bunz asked.

Joe set down a box of groceries and paused to remember. "One of them, he was huge. You wouldn't miss him in a crowd. And the other one, I guess he smiled too much. Gave me the creeps."

Bunz hefted a box of coffee down toward the deck. Joe reached up for it and said, "Some reason you asking?"

Bunz gave him a narrow look. "I need a reason?"

"Ha!" Joe saw that the rabbit had his cop face on. He glanced over at Bongo. Bongo shrugged. "So, what do you want to know?"

"What they were doing."

"Wasting Guys' time mostly. Asking questions and trying to charter a boat on the cheap."

"Questions about Murkey's?"

"No, no, don't think so. Asked about the boats, where we go, when it's busy, and my favorite: could they ride along for free. Clowns!" he said with disgust. "We left to fuel the boat, so they didn't get around to us."

"Ida mentioned that you thought they might be real estate Guys."

"No, that's what Ida thought."

Bunz watched Joe carry the supply boxes below.

Ida said one thing, Joe said the opposite. This is going nowhere. What else is there to ask?

"C'mon Joe," Pops called out from the wheelhouse. The engines of the *Fishy Lady* fired up. "Time to get along." He put the boat in gear and she pulled up against her mooring lines.

Joe snagged the stern mooring line as Bunz tossed it down and said, "Check with the wharf seagulls. You know how they are."

"Had that thought," Bunz said dryly. He untied the bow line and tossed it down.

Pops took the boat briefly out of gear; Joe took off the spring line, and Pops eased the boat away from the slip. As the boat turned, Bunz called out, "Did they get their boat ride?" The noise from the accelerating engines rumbled over Joe's reply.

Fishy Lady was the last boat out. Her dim shape faded into the fog and reflections of the dock lights squiggled as the boat's wake rolled through the water. The sound of foghorns drifted through the dark.

Bongo jigged up and down. He was cold and tired. The coffee had worn off. The cookies seemed a long time ago. "Geez, Bunz. Hamms said, Ida said, Joe said." He danced back and forth on his paws. "It's like I'm chasing my tail."

Bunz scowled. The jigging dog was annoying. "Should have asked Joe if he had any idea where those two were holed up."

Bongo gave Bunz a sideways look and shivered. "A dead end, huh? I'm thinking maybe we take a break."

Bunz considered the dog for a long moment. No help at all. "Yeah. Go ahead."

He watched Bongo trot off and let out a disgusted sigh. *What now?* He looked around.

If moose are in this neighborhood, Silver Dollar Sid might know.

At this idea, Bunz felt a surge of energy.

And if they're staying at The Lodge Motel, Silver D. will give me a little look inside their room in exchange for a little folding green.

He turned inland. But three steps along, he remembered. Silver D. didn't work nights anymore.

Confound it!

He glanced up at the dark sky. Still too early for seagulls.

5: A Moose at Murkey's

Back at Murkey's, Ida did a last look-around. After Webbs left, no one had come in. She re-mopped the floor where the Guys had left wet paw prints. The tables were all set, condiments full. Clean plates, cups, glasses and flatware were stacked high. Napkin dispensers full. Everything was ready for the morning rush.

Soon there would be a crowd ordering fresh donuts and coffee, pie and coffee, bacon and pancakes, tea with toast from the Acme bread company, eggs and potatoes, all those good things that made Murkey's a breakfast heaven.

She poured herself a cup of coffee and sat at the counter. Hamms' baking filled the diner with the scent of hot, fresh pastry. Ida sighed. She could never get enough of the fragrance of fresh baking.

During the Sugar Ban, she'd lost her best job ever, decorating fancy cakes and pastry. Her boss was one of the ones who had refused to use the fake stuff. So many businesses had shut down and many Guys lost their jobs. It was a relief when they discovered how toxic the sugar substitutes were and made real sugar legal again! But that great job was long gone.

The clock ticked. Three a.m. She was tired. Her long days started with bartending at the Old Anchor and finished with the late shift at the diner. She was ready to go home, but it wasn't time yet. She knew she was lucky to have two jobs she could easily juggle, and the money she earned from them allowed her to live in the city instead of having to commute for hours every day. The free meal at Murkey's was a daily bonus.

Over the past few weeks, she'd been working up the nerve to talk to Hamms about letting her decorate some of his donuts. Or even let her bake some fancy cookies—see how the customers liked them. If only she could determine the best way to bring it up. Like all bakers, that hamster was prickly. But underneath, she felt, he was a good Guy. And she hoped the good Guy would give her a break.

Why not ask him now? What was the worst he could say?

She turned on the buzzer for the front door, took a deep breath, and pushed open the kitchen door. She had to pause. Mayhem! Hamms was having a busy morning and the kitchen looked a mess. Dirty pots and pans everywhere. In the middle of the mess, the hamster was grousing to himself. She smiled when she saw there was no Doc to be seen.

Bet he's in the back, out of the line of fire, she thought.

She wished herself luck and said, "Hey, Hamms. I'm done out front. Need any help here?"

The hamster looked at her as though he had never seen her before. He was wondering why he had decided to overdo it this morning and make three kinds of pie. It was getting late, and he needed a clean bowl to beat the egg whites for the lemon meringue pie. But he'd used up all the bowls! He'd have to stop and wash one!

Ach! He was losing his rhythm. He hated that. A kitchen had to have a certain rhythm or the food became flat. And here was that Ida. She usually had the good sense to leave him alone when he was baking. His eyes snapped into focus and he stared at her.

"You know what?" he asked. "See this bowl right here?" He pointed to a counter full of dirty bowls. "This one?" He picked up a big stainless-steel mixing bowl. "I need this bowl clean. Clean, clean, super clean. For egg whites. You know how clean that is?"

Ida nodded. "Zero grease," she said as the hamster kept talking.

"Let's see if you can clean that real good. And dry it. With a clean cloth. No grease! None! I got Danish ready to come out of the ovens. I got pies to put in the ovens. I got meringue to make." Hamms stalked over to his ovens and peeked at the Danish.

Ida took the big bowl over to the pot sink. With the bowl clean and dry, she turned to see Hamms taking beautiful cheese and apricot Danish out of the ovens. Without saying anything, she put the bowl over near his work area and began to gather up all the dirty pots, pans, and bowls.

Hamms glanced over at her.

This rabbit, she's got a steady, quiet air about her, he thought. Not one of those chatterbox-types. She even stacked bowls in the sink quietly.

"Don't wash those now," he snapped. "Just put 'em in to soak. Let these Danish cool a few minutes, then put them on the display trays. I gotta get these meringue pies in the oven. Then we'll cook donuts. Oil will be ready soon."

Ida smiled and opened her mouth to say something, but then shut it again.

He said 'we', she thought. *'We'll cook donuts'.*

Pots and pans soaked in the big, soapy pot sink. Pastries cooled. Hamms cracked eggs and whipped egg whites. Ida wiped counters and swept the floor.

She called out, "I'm taking this tray out front. It'll smell good for the early customers."

And for me.

She grabbed a tray of Danish and backed her way through the kitchen door. Just then the front door buzzer buzzed. She turned and almost dropped the warm pastries in surprise.

A big moose stood just inside the diner, looking around. It was the big moose from the Old Anchor! He gave her a dull stare. She let the kitchen door swing closed behind her.

She said an automatic "Good morning. Have a seat, please. I'll just put this down and be right with you."

Without speaking, he took a stool at the counter. To the back of her head he said, "Coffee," in the deep, moosey voice she remembered from the bar. She set the tray of pastries near the display case. Her nerves jittered.

If I yell, Hamms or Doc will hear me. Then she paused and thought, *Don't be wimpy, girl! See what happens first.*

She turned around and pasted on a smile.

"Coffee or 'spresso?" She couldn't keep the little quaver from her voice.

Irritation flashed in his eyes. He loomed, even bigger than she remembered.

Unconsciously she moved back a step.

"Jes' plain coffee, awright? Black."

At the Old Anchor, when the Moose had been on the other side of the stalwart oak bar, she felt safe. With just a little plastic lunch counter between them, not so much.

The coffee cups rattled as she grabbed one. She let the coffee slowly fill the cup and took the moment to steady her nerves.

Maybe I can get some info for Bunz. Start simple, like 'I see you made it down here' or 'Where's your friend tonight?'

Behind her, she heard him take in a big breath and let it out noisily.

"Smells darn good in here," he said.

As she placed the cup and saucer gently on the counter, she concentrated on keeping her paws steady. She made herself look up at him, right in the eye, and shined a bright smile. "Sugar?"

The fumes of stale moose breath flowed into her sensitive nose. She spontaneously snuffed it out and edged back.

"Nah." He sipped his coffee.

"We bake our own pastries here," she said with professional cheer. "Those are fresh Danish, just out of the oven! Can I get you one?"

Moose shook his head in the negative.

I don't think he remembers me.

"Ya know what?" Moose broke in on her thoughts. "I remember when this joint used ta have great pie. Real great pie." He looked down the counter at the pie display. His voice got dreamy for a moment. He didn't see the startled look cross Ida's face. "They had this blueberry pie."

He knows this place! she thought. *Back at the Old Anchor he pretended not to.*

"Reminded me a' home, that pie did, where I grew up." Moose refocused on her. "Ya still got pie? Blueberry pie? That pie was good as what my ma used ta make."

She was too flustered to remember what pie they had. She walked toward the pie display and composed herself.

"Right now, we have, uh, cherry and banana creme. What can I get you?"

"Naw, naw. Nope," Moose said. "None a' that. All I want," his eyes gleamed, "yes sir, is some a that bluuueberry pie! Ain't had any in years."

"Well, the baker is here. He may be making blueberry pie today."

She was at the kitchen door when Moose's deep voice rumbled again. "Is Towtruck back there ta-night?"

She was confused. "You need a tow truck?"

Moose frowned. "Towtruck! Towtruck the dishwasher! He still around?"

"Towtruck the dishwasher? I-I don't know. But I haven't worked here very long. I'll go ask and be right back."

The kitchen door swung closed behind her.

He knew someone who worked here? What's going on? She realized she was holding her breath. She let it out in a whoosh.

Hamms looked up from the deep fat fryer, annoyed to see her just standing there, breathing, as though she didn't know he was waiting for her.

"You ready to do donuts or what?" he asked, peeved. He checked the oil thermometer. Perfect temperature for donuts.

"Hamms, Hamms!" She hurried over to him.

"What!?"

"Hamms! That big moose—that I saw at the bar? He's out there. Drinking coffee."

"So?" said Hamms. *So what,* he thought. *These donuts are ready to fry now!*

He swung the hopper of soft dough over the bubbling pot of oil.

"He's asking about blueberry pie and someone named Towtruck."

Hamms said nothing as he concentrated on laying the soft dough gently into the hot oil. No automatic donut cookers for him. As the donuts sizzled, Hamms said, "Towtruck. Dishwasher here. Five-six years ago. Maybe longer."

He watched the donuts dance in the bubbling oil. The first sides were turning golden brown.

Hamms cooking donuts the old-school way.

Out front, Moose sipped his coffee. He looked around. Place looked the same.

What a dump, he thought. But he was relieved that nothing had changed. *So I get back inta the kitchen, see if th' trapdoor's still there, with that stair down ta the water. Get that waitress and that baker outta the way. Make a quick deal with Towtruck. Maybe even finish this ta-night.*

Moose pictured the underside of the diner. He figured he was sitting no more than forty feet from a bundle he could live on for years. It was good ta be back.

Hamms flipped the donuts to cook on the other side. Ida watched, distressed she wasn't helping. But that moose was out there waiting.

"What about blueberry pie?" she asked Hamms again.

Hamms did not look up. "What about it?"

"Did you make blueberry today? The moose is asking for it."

"Do you see blueberry? No, you do not! You see lemon meringue, apple, and chocolate cream." He shook his head. "Don't ask me why."

"Too bad."

"What do you mean, too bad?" he snapped. He pushed the donuts around to be sure they browned evenly. "These are done. If you're going to help, now's the time, before they cool too much."

He dipped the golden donuts out of the hot oil and set them on wire racks to drain.

"I'll do it. I will! Can I just tell him we'll have blueberry pie tomorrow?"

Hamms looked closely at Ida, exasperated. *She's worried about tomorrow and here I got donuts need to be sugared now!* Somebody had to take charge of this moose situation!

"Look here," he said. "Powder sugar these. Granulated on those. Glazed when I get back. I'll take care of your moose!" Hamms wiped his hands on the towel hanging at his waist and headed for the door.

Ida's eyes widened. There was no way for her to stop him from annoying the customer. She picked up the powdered sugar.

As Hamms pushed open the door into the diner, he looked back at Ida. She had begun sprinkling sugar. He saw she had a good rhythm, no waste motion.

"Hey!" He walked back over and grabbed a plate. "Give me a couple of those." *And they think I can't deal with the public,* he thought.

Moose was staring at the kitchen door when the hamster came through. Hamms stopped for a minute, startled when he saw how large the moose was. Moose watched this. He loved it when his size made Guys stop and take a look. Especially when they had to look way, way up, like this runty hamster did.

Hamms put the donuts down on the counter near Moose and noticed his empty cup. "Get you a refill there?"

"Huh," said Moose. He pushed his coffee cup across the counter. *If this hamster's all I gotta deal with, th' caper's a done deal,* he thought.

Hamms refilled Moose's cup and poured a

cup for himself. He turned and set Moose's cup on the saucer.

"Care for a fresh donut?"

Moose shook his big head 'no'.

Hamms shrugged. "I'm the baker here. I understand you have a question about pie."

Moose's heavy eyes lit up. "The baker, huh? So, you make that blueberry pie I ate that was so good, maybe ten years ago it woulda been."

"Well, you are probably right, if it was ten years ago. I've been here close to twelve years. Yes, that probably was my pie." Hamms puffed up little at the implied praise.

"That was some good-eatin' pie. Real good." Moose set his cup down with a snap. Coffee sloshed into the saucer and splashed across the counter. "I dreamed about that pie. Yes sir, I sure did!"

Hamms swelled a little more. "Well now. Made a good impression, did it? I'm making blueberry tomorrow, if you're interested. I'm usually done with the baking around seven. If you could come back after that—"

Moose nearly smiled. "I jus' might do that. I jus' might. After seven, eh? You know," Moose shifted on his stool, "this Guy I use ta know, Towtruck. He's not back there ta-night?"

"No, he's not. He hasn't been here for some time. Friend of yours?"

Moose grunted. "Yeah, you could say that."

He leaned forward. "He tol' me once there was some kind a' ol' trap door in this joint somewheres. I never seen it, a-course. That true?"

"Yes. Back in the kitchen. It interests you?"

Too many personal questions. Moose glowered. Hamms' fur bristled at the unfriendly response. The front door buzzed. Moose tensed and turned to look. Ida came out from the kitchen with a plate of donuts. She glanced at Hamms and the moose.

Oh great, she thought. She choked back a nervous laugh at the faces they were making.

A Guy in fishing boots slid into a chair by the window.

Gettin' crowded, Moose thought. He turned back to Hamms.

Hamms said, "Matter of fact, we had that hatch open a couple of hours ago."

Moose's eyes drilled into Hamms. "Open?" he growled.

"Sure," Hamms said blandly. "We heard something banging around. Pried it open for a look."

Ida flinched as Moose rose off his stool, looming over Hamms.

Omigod, she thought. *Here we go.*

The hamster drew himself up to his full height. *This moose is a little sensitive,* he thought.

"Then what?" Moose demanded.

"It was something the tide brought in. Banging pretty hard against the pier, it was."

"What was?"

"Driftwood." Hamms' sharp teeth showed a little as he stifled a grin.

Moose snorted. The door buzzer went off again. The moose jerked around to eyeball the new customer.

Way too crowded now, Moose, he thought. *This ain't th' time.* He tossed a few coins on the counter and faded out the door.

Hamms looked down at the change. "Will you look at this, Ida. Seventy-five cents for coffee, with refills! Where's that Guy been?"

Outside, beyond the light from the diner window, Moose paused in the cool air and took a slow look around. Empty.

For one bad minute, he'd been sure the runty hamster was gonna tell him they'd found that dumb Smilin' and that mouthy dog floatin' dead under the diner. Or worse, alive. But no. Those two were goners fer sure. Only bad thing, the dog had gone down with his $285. But he'd have plenty of cash soon!

Time ta get back ta Bill's.

From habit, Moose merged in with the shadows. Funny how growing up in the woods paid off.

He thought of his Pa—one moment of

carelessness, and hunters had gunned him down and dragged him off. After that, Ma had made durn sure he learned to fade into the background at all times. Turned out it was a useful skill anywhere.

And this fog, it was a blessing fer sure. He liked how it hid everything. Things would work out, just not how he planned. One thing going for him now: he was on his own again. That loud-mouth Smilin' Moose had turned into a blister. He was a city moose. Knew nuthin'. And two moose together, Guys remember that. Alone was better.

The slightest tingle from his antlers, and he paused for a slow look around. Deserted. Moose began to calm down.

Zero for two, he thought as he walked along. Looked like Towtruck didn't work there no more, and the fish boat plan had fizzled.

But third time's the charm. Gotta be.

Why was Moose so confident that G.G. and Smilin' Moose were goners? What catastrophe had struck the *Sea Dog* just a few foggy hours ago?

6: A Moose in the Fog

The *Sea Dog's* engines idled; the boat rocked gently in the night, two hundred yards off Pier 13. At the same time, Bunz and the card players were approaching Murkey's Diner.

Moose was alone aboard the *Sea Dog*, standing watch at the helm. Where was Captain G.G.? Absent. Smilin' Moose? Also absent. Moose had it figured: high tide was the time to reach the loot he'd stashed under Murkey's ten long years ago. G.G. would row, Smilin' would grab the stash. Easy-peasy and gone. A few minutes earlier, Moose had ordered G.G. to take her little skiff off the roof of the pilothouse and row Smilin' under the pier.

"No way," she snapped. "Did you happen to check a tide table? Don't you know the tide's extra high tonight? There's not enough room to get underneath. You couldn't pay me enough to try."

But the hefty rifle he pulled from his duffle bag convinced her otherwise.

So, off the wrathful dog rowed, the short, unhappy moose sitting in the stern. Very quickly the little *Pup* disappeared into the dense fog. Moose's high-powered rifle scope was of scant use to track them. The boat's binoculars were no better. But Moose stood and looked after them anyway.

G.G. rows off into the fog with a reluctant Smilin'.

Life's already tough enough, he groused to himself. *Then I had ta get locked away those ten freakin' years. Only me, bum luck Moose, would get popped just before the Sugar Ban was repealed. I need this stash more than ever.*

After ten minutes, he saw a fuzzy blotch of light. *Aw-right! Smilin' turned on th' flashlight. They must be there.*

The bright spot bobbed around, but after some minutes he could no longer see it. And now they had been gone longer than Moose had reckoned. Had that big mouthy dog been right? Was it unsafe? He began to consider. What if those two weren't coming back? That would leave him all alone on the boat, and not just for a brief wait.

Poof! His confidence went dry. He froze. Just like that! Panic flooded his brain and jammed it up. His lungs quit. His chest got tight.

But then, like the good ol' days back home, his Ma's voice came to him, soundin' just like she did when she taught him survival in the woods.

"Start basic, Moose," she said. "What do you know, right here, right now?"

He took in a breath and slowly examined the wheelhouse. That Big Dog, she kept her boat good. Everything neat and handy and in working order. He noticed that first thing. This wasn't his first fish boat, no sir. And fish boats were all alike, right? This fish boat was like all the other fish boats he had been on, smuggling sugar night after night. He stood a little taller in the wheelhouse.

Back then, out in open water, while the captain took a break, Moose would take a spell at the helm. He enjoyed those hours, watching for ship traffic on the radar, keeping the boat on course. He had felt like Sprinkhels sailing his private yacht.

He took another strong breath.

OK, Moose. This fish boat is just like them others. Nuthin' new here. Throttles, steering, compass, radar. Ya already been out here fer thirty minutes, keepin' the boat in position, no problem. Ya got this, boyo. Quit yer worryin'.

But where the heck were those two inchworms? He tried again to peer through the windshield—but it dripped with fog. He stepped out of the wheelhouse and looked toward the pier.

Nuthin'! If only the durn fog would lift, just a little bit.

If he took the boat in any closer to the pier, he might get pushed onto the pilings by the tide currents. If he kept his distance, well, the boat had a searchlight, but if he turned it on and someone saw him—Moose snorted! They might think he needed help. He did not need no stinkin' help.

So durn foggy, they could be rowin' back this minute and I wouldn't know. Not till they bumped inta th' boat. Should I a' paid attention ta that yappin' dog? Naw. Then this whole trip ta grab the stash would be fer nothin'.

He waited a few minutes longer, but he had that bad feeling—the kind that sticks in yer gut when plans go sideways.

He thought back to the ship's wake that rolled by after those two had rowed off. When the wake passed underneath him, the fish boat barely bobbed. But the wave kinda rolled up under the pier pretty hard. He heard it crash up against the bottom of the pier decking, loud enough to be heard over the idling boat engines. That's when he'd seen the flashlight blink out. Since then, nothing.

He studied the radar. Nuthin' on the screen but him. He thought for a moment. His stealth hidin' place fer the stolen sugar money was turning into a big pain in the antlers. It had seemed foolproof at the time—tuck it under the pier, sealed up tight, safe until he could sneak back and grab it.

Moose had a good laugh on Sprinkhels Junior that night. Instead of moving Junior's sugar for chump change, Moose made off with Junior's fair share of the big money. It was just back wages, the way Moose saw it.

And the gag? It was Junior's money, hid under Junior's diner. Unlaundered bootleggin' money, so ol' Junior couldn't even report it stolen. Ha-ha.

But right now, ain't quite so funny.

It's so stinkin' foggy, no one else out here 'cept me and that tomfool ship. If I can't see them two, then fer sure no one else did. If they was flipped into this cold water, likely they was dead by now. If that's th' way th' dice is rollin', I need me a new plan. OK. What's my next move then?

Moose considered his plight. Number one, he had to get himself to shore. Put the boat in somewheres it wouldn't get noticed. Which way should he go, in all this fog? North, south, east?

Hey! Moose smiled in the dark. South, right? Mister Fancy-Pants Swellhead Sprinkhels Junior had that handy little yacht club south a' the Ferry Building.

Moose's smiled widened. Mister F. P. Sprinkhels could just help his old pal Moose out once again.

I motor down ta th' yacht club, dump th' boat an' decamp. Perfect! This time a' night, who's ta know?

Moose turned the boat south and made way slowly along the city front.

Where was Towtruck anyway? He was a good angle to get at the stash, if he was still around. What about Bill the Bum? He might know sumthin'. Yeah! Plus, maybe Bill will let me crash at his place fer a few days.

OK! New plan. Not going back ta that cheap-sleep motel by the tourist wharf. Not going back to that part of town, period. Shoulda played it closer ta the vest, Moose ol' boy. Ya got a little too giddy bein' out and about after so many years. Too many Guys saw ya with Smilin', pro'lly saw ya chartering this dang bad-luck boat.

Off on his starboard side, Moose saw lights from the Ferry Building ghost by.

Better pay attention, Moose. Comin' up ta that Bay Bridge. Don't want ta run into no stinkin' bridge tower, like Guys have been known ta do. An' that yacht basin, it ain't too far south a' the bridge.

He peered into the fog. It hadn't seemed so terrible bad when G.G. was driving. He squinted. Nothin' but nothin' outside the wind screen. Where were those navigation lights on the bridge?

He studied the radar display. What scale was it set on?

One and a half miles. OK. The lumpy green mass there on the right side of the dark screen, that was the shore, he knew that. *And my boat is the dot in the middle, with the radar sweep cycling around it. The green line across the top of the screen—could that be the bridge?*

Gad. Must be. What else could it be? And them little green dots, les'see, they're not moving. I'm the only one out here moving. Gonna call them dots the buoys as mark the bridge tower. So I go between 'em. If I go real slow and hit something, it won't be too bad.

He eased back on the throttles to slow the engines a little more. The high tide had begun to ebb and the boat struggled against the outflowing current that rushed north toward the Golden Gate and the sea.

Fog and more fog. Nothing visible outside his windows. He looked again at the radar. The green mass of shore appeared a lot closer. The currents were pushing the boat toward land. His heart pounded. His grip tightened on the wheel as he turned a few degrees to port. The green shore moved back away from his position.

Good. OK! This'll work, Moose. This'll work.

Fog dripped down the windows. He took a quick look around for the wiper switch, but in the dark of the wheelhouse, he couldn't find it.

Wipers won't make no rotten difference in this pea soup anyways.

The boat engines throbbed.

He breathed in and let it out slowly.

That's what Ma had said: Always breathe, boy. Don't get lost in the panic.

He wished she was here now—to see how good her boy was doing.

He knew he was nearing the massive Bay Bridge. He checked the radar again. From the top of the screen, the green bar that represented the bridge had moved down to his position at the center of the screen. He could see nothing outside his windows, but on the radar screen, the green image of the bridge crept over the dot of his boat's position. He gripped the throttles and braced himself. Was he going to hit?

He stood by, ready to take the boat out of gear if he did. His eyes couldn't resist trying to bore through the fog outside the windows, but there was nothing to see. Very slowly, the invisible bridge passed over him as the green bar moved toward the screen bottom. He shook himself. He was still making way! He eased the throttle ahead.

Yer awful good, my Moose. Ya got clear water now. Take a good breath, boyo. Take a good deep breath and let's head fer that yacht basin!

He wished he could see something, anything, outside the boat windows. But he could not. So. If he couldn't see, how was he going to recognize that yacht basin when he got near it? He thought for a moment of the many times he'd slipped in and out of the basin on different sugar boats.

Ahh, yes! I remember: there was a seawall, parallel ta shore, not sticking out like th' piers did. None a' the other piers had a seawall like that, jus' Pier 40. Look for a skinny parallel green line, ol' Moose. That's yer sign.

On the radar screen, a finger of pier jutted greenly out from the blob of shoreline, reaching out into the bay. Then a nub of something began to extend down from the top of the screen. It got longer. A long, skinny line grew toward his position. There! That was it! The good ol' seawall. That had to be it!

Eyes on the radar screen, he steered toward the entrance to the yacht basin. As he got closer, the opening between the seawall and Pier 40 looked much too narrow for his wide fish boat. He closed his eyes to remember going in. An opening—not too big, not too small, maybe 50 feet wide—off the end of Pier 40. Boats entered the yacht basin by going between the seawall and the pier.

He'd been in that harbor many times. Was it always this narrow? He'd have to trust his memory and steer by the radar. He slowed to bare steerage way and cautiously headed toward the narrow gap, eyes locked onto the radar screen. He slid open the portside window, praying for the seawall to appear through the fog. Praying to see something!

He couldn't slow down any more or he would stop. The engine rumbled; the boat rolled gently. The radar screen showed his position approaching the gap. He felt as though his eyeballs were going to pop out of his head as he strained to see.

"Please, please let me see something," he muttered.

Then vaguely, no more than two feet from the boat, he saw a ghost outline. The seawall? Or nothing. He squeezed his eyes shut and popped them open again.

Wait—no, yes! It was the seawall! And he was heading straight for it! His heart pounded. He jerked the throttles back and hiked the wheel to starboard. The boat turned, but not quite fast enough. He felt the hull thud against the seawall on his port side. Thump! Scrape! That heart-stopping stutter when a boat hits something solid. But she kept moving! The good ol' boat kept movin'!

"OK, OK. Breathe, Moose, keep breathin', buddy boy."

He set the throttles ahead slow and straightened his course parallel to the seawall. "C'mon, Moose!" he whispered. "Almost there."

With one eye on the radar and one on the blurry form in the fog, he entered the yacht harbor. On his right, the end of Pier 40 ghosted past and he was in the empty patch of water that led to the yacht berths. He took the boat out of gear and ducked out of the wheelhouse to look around.

A dim row of docked sailboats formed on his left. On his right, the grey misty shape of the pier shed materialized. Now if he could just find an empty berth to leave the fish boat at.

The boat drifted to a stop. He was almost alongside a narrow float that ran parallel to the pier shed.

What did he see? A big empty nuthin' tied alongside the float! Was it true? He squeezed his tired eyes shut and looked again.

Too good ta be true, Ma! Yer boy is a lucky moose ta-night!

Back at the wheel and back in gear, he guided a barely-moving boat toward the float. At the last minute, he put the engines into reverse to check her forward motion, then shifted back into neutral and stepped out to the deck.

He grabbed a mooring line, flipped the eye onto a boat cleat and crouched by the rail. This part he had done many times. A little bump! Down he jumped onto the float. He hoped no one heard the snap his hooves made hitting the wood decking. Holding the line tight, he walked along the floating dock, peering around for a cleat.

Found one! Fer Pete's sake! Almost tripped on it.

He took a half turn around the cleat, pulled the stern against the float and made the line off quickly. As she fetched up against the line, the bow began to swing away from the float. Before she could swing too far, he leaped back onto the deck, and walked to the bow. He attached another line to the bow cleat, then hustled back into the wheelhouse. Pulling gently against his stern spring line, he fussed with the rudder and throttles until he got the bow to swing back toward the float. Back on the float, he made the bow line fast. A little tangled maybe, but good enough.

Done. Phew!

He examined his handiwork.

Looky looky here. Better 'n I thought I was. Ya still got it, Moose ol' son. Ma would be proud!

Back on the boat, Moose turned off the engines and the generator, gathered his stuff, and made his quickest getaway ever. It took real technique not to let his hooves clomp on the wooden float as he headed to shore. He pushed through the security gate and eased it closed.

It felt good to be back on dry land. He listened. Just light traffic in the distance. He looked around as best he could.

Durn fog's almost worse here than it was on the water.

Out by the street, he paused to get his bearings. Where was he? Still north of Sipp's Creek and Bill the Bum's houseboat.

I'll just walk south till I run into good ol' Sipp's Creek, turn inland, and I'm there.

Though why they called that crusty canal a creek he didn't know. It was nothing at all like the woodland creeks he played in as a young moose. Too much concrete and trash. But so what. If his luck held, Bill would be home. He could drop his gear, maybe get a line on Towtruck.

The main thing was, he had ta get back ta Murkey's before it got busy. He could hoof it ta the diner now, but he was carrying too much gear. Among other things, his big rifle. Not so good ta be seen waltzing around with that!

That chump Smilin' and that uppity dog? Hopefully they was done for. If not, speed was his best bet.

Moose hoofed it into the fog.

7: Doc Rows Home

Just a few hours after Moose high-tailed it out of Murkey's front door, the back door off the kitchen opened. Doc stepped onto the pier and sniffed the sweet damp air of the early-morning bay. He looked at the weather: still foggy. No wind. The fog had lifted to around twenty feet above water level.

The moose had come and gone from the diner, but for Doc the presence of a moose was trivial. Life was what it was. If something happened to Murkey's, he'd just have to look for another job.

But not tonight. Tonight, business had been slow and Hamms told Doc to push off early. The tiger smiled: leaving early and tomorrow was his day off! That's what was on his mind.

Now for the best part of his day. Rowing home. They all teased him about rowing to work in his tiny skiff; every other boat and ship traversing the bay was larger than his. But rowing suited him. Out on the water, the city faded away, and his troubles with it. The beat-up old rowboat might not be a beauty, but she was light and handy and easy to row. He called her his *Prescription*, because he always felt good when he was out rowing. No motors, no noise. Just him, his oars, and the water.

He set down the bag of two-day-old pastries he was taking home and took a few minutes to stretch and touch his toes. He worked his shoulders around to loosen them up. He walked to the edge of the pier and looked down. The tide was still low. Near the bottom of the pier access ladder, his little blue skiff bobbed at the end of its painter. The tide was so low, the whole length of the painter had stretched out.

The tiger hooked the bag of pastries over his shoulder, untied the boat's long painter, and holding it in one paw, worked his way down the ladder. Pausing just above the water, he looped the painter around the ladder and hauled the boat in close. He tossed the pastry bag down, un-looped the painter and made a handy leap to the center of the skiff. It barely rocked as he landed softly. A push against the old bent ladder and off he floated.

He sat still for a moment, enjoying that splendid feeling of floating free. Then he deftly coiled the painter in the bow, stowed the pastries in a waterproof bag, and unshipped the oars. Wrapped in leather, the oarlocks made no sound as he leaned into the oars. With his easy, long stroke, the boat gathered speed and slid past the end of Pier 13. He turned into a southerly course, along The Embarcadero, towards Sipp's Creek and home.

He was alone. His whiskers relaxed as he dug the oars into the water and pulled. He was close enough to shore to hear the water lap against the wall of The Embarcadero. The gentle sound always reminded him of the lake where he had learned to row when he was a tiger cub.

Every few minutes he paused to look around. No flotsam in sight, but you never knew what you might find in the bay. He kept his eyes open for salvage. He'd never had to buy a boat fender. There were plenty that had fallen off the boats of clowns who didn't know enough to stow them when they were underway.

With the tide running high, there was an improved chance of encountering a waterlogged timber or a derelict piece of sunken boat. The piling that had clonked the diner just hours earlier might still be lurking nearby.

Sunrise was near, but fog still concealed the sky, making it too dark to see much beneath the piers. At Pier 11, he could make out nothing in the shadows. As he passed the tip of the pier, he turned to look from a different angle. And far back in the forest of pilings, his eye caught the blur of something large and white. He held the oars still for a moment. The gloom was difficult to penetrate. Hard to say what he was seeing. Had it moved? He rowed closer.

Geez! He squinted. *What was that? Was that a groan?*

He didn't want to row under the pier. But definitely, it looked like someone was in a skiff, half sunk at the edge of the water. And soon, he knew, the tide was going to flood back into the bay.

He worked his boat nearer. "Hey! Hey there!" he called out.

A big white dog lifted its head. Round black eyes looked toward him uncertainly.

"Hey! Big Dog! Can you hear me? Hey, you!"

G.G. took hold of the side of her skiff. This was her skiff alright, but why was it filled with water? She tried to sit up, but shivered instead and felt herself swoon. Her stomach clenched as she felt the boat scrape against the rocks beneath. Water sloshed around her paws. The oars seemed to have floated away.

This had to be a bad dream.

"Hey! Hello there!" Doc shouted. "You're under the pier here and the tide's coming in!" The pier pilings crowded around as Doc rowed his boat closer.

The dog tried to focus on the little tiger in his little boat as he neared. Her eyes weren't working right. She squeezed them shut and tried to focus again, shivering steadily.

"Can you climb into my boat?" he called to her.

She waved a paw at the tiger and tried to stand up. The skiff wobbled on the rocks. The world began to spin. Water sloshed around. She sagged back onto the seat and closed her eyes, waiting for the spinning to stop. Why was she so shaky? Her head ached terribly.

"Hey-hey there! Don't go to sleep." The tiger might have been small but he had a big voice.

G.G. opened an eye and tried again to focus on the bobbing tiger.

"Can you come any closer?" she called out weakly.

"OK, a little bit." Doc maneuvered his boat closer to the dog's boat. "I don't want to bottom out when you get in."

"You won't." She stood up slowly and put one paw on the gunwale. To encourage him she said, "There's a little drop-off right here, and I'll step into the center as best I can."

Doc worked the stern of his boat in closer to the dog, who half-stood in the middle of her stove-in boat. G.G. set one paw down in the center of Doc's boat and lifted the other off the bottom of her sunken skiff. Deftly she shifted her balance and transferred over to Doc's boat. His mighty little vessel took the load gallantly. Dripping wet, the big dog settled onto the aft seat. Only a few inches of freeboard remained.

Doc leaned into the oars and they zigzagged around the pilings, back to open water. The wet dog was heavy. Water ran off her fur and pooled in the bottom of the boat. As he propelled the loaded boat toward the Ferry Building, he glanced at his watch. Still too early to worry about the morning ferryboats. Doc knew the rule of tonnage: any boat bigger than yours, you give them right of way. Doc's personal rule: avoid all vessels at all times. As the Ferry Building slid by, the tiger began to get hot from the exertion of rowing such a large load.

"Watch it a second, bud. I gotta shake off some water," G.G. warned Doc. Doc shut his eyes and kept rowing. Wet dog water flew as she shook off as much of the bay as she could without capsizing the little boat.

"OK. Done."

Doc opened his eyes and looked over at the wet, straggly dog. G.G. shivered and looked around.

"Where we headed?" she asked. Her keen ears heard no boat engines; no fog signals sounded from boats under way in the fog. Just the tiger's steady breathing as they made way south.

Doc thought a moment. "Well, unless you think different, I'm heading to my sailboat over in Sipp's Creek. You can dry off there."

G.G. shrugged. Until she knew where her fish boat was, she couldn't think of a better idea. And right now, she didn't feel too good. Her head pounded. She winced as she found a sore lump behind her ear. She probed it gently.

Doc watched as his passenger put a paw up to rub her head.

"Are you OK?" he asked.

G.G. made no reply. In the bilge she spotted a sponge stowed in the corner. She picked it up and methodically sopped up the water that had drained off her into the boat and squeezed it back into the bay. When the bilge was dry, she remembered to pat the pocket where she had put the charter money. At least that was still there.

She asked, "What's the time?"

"About four-fifteen."

"In the morning."

"Yep."

"You live in Sipp's Creek?"

"Yep."

"I guess that's as good a place as any."

Doc rowed on in silence. This was not what he had planned for his day off.

Twenty-five minutes later they reached the mouth of Sipp's Creek, slid under the two old bridges that crossed it, and headed for a row of houseboats strung along the south side. In quick order, Doc had his little skiff tied to a cleat on a floating walkway and they climbed aboard his sailboat.

Doc unlocked the hatch to the cabin and led the way below. Out on deck, G.G. gave herself a good shake. As the water flew off, her world started spinning. She stumbled and grabbed at the sail winch to keep from falling.

Darn it. I don't have time for this.

Gingerly she stepped into the hatch and descended the ladder to the cabin.

It was a snug little boat for a small tiger but a tight fit for a large dog. G.G. ducked her head and sat on a banquette covered in fake leather. At least her wet dog butt wouldn't stain it.

Doc saw G.G. shiver in the chill air. He set the pastries down and said, "Hold on a sec. I'll get you a towel." He looked at the size of the dog and added, "Maybe a couple of towels. I'll get this heater going. Then I'll make coffee."

G.G. looked around as she waited. The boat may have needed paint on the outside, but the inside was shipshape and Bristol fashion. The wood trim shone, everything was stowed; the banquette was comfortable.

Doc handed her two clean towels. She rubbed her fur as dry as she could and folded the towels to sit on so they could sop up any extra water seeping down her butt.

She sagged back on the canvas cushions. Her head ached something terrible. She massaged her forehead, trying to calm the pain. The heater warmed and she held out her paws to toast them. As the heat penetrated, she began to feel drowsy.

Doc kept an eye on her as he bustled about his compact little galley. "By the way, my name's Doc."

G.G. opened one eye and looked over at him. "Doc. OK, Doc. Pleased to meet you."

As the smell of brewing coffee filled the air, G.G. felt a little faint. She heard the gurgle as Doc filled two mugs. "Wow, that smells good! Would you happen to have a little taste of something to put into that coffee?"

Doc set the two mugs on the counter and reached under the sink. He held aloft a bottle of brandy. "You wouldn't mean like this, would you?"

The sad-looking dog perked up at the sight

of brandy. Into the mugs he added a splash of brandy. "Sugar or cream?" he asked.

"Sugar would work for me," she said. "Not too much."

Doc handed her the coffee. She held it in her paws and soaked in the warmth from the sides of the cup. She sniffed the aroma and took a tiny, hot sip.

"Ahhhhh." She leaned back.

"Are you hungry?" Doc asked. "I brought home some pastries."

"No, thank you. I don't think I can eat right now. Just coffee."

Doc took his cup and settled himself on the opposite banquette. He studied the dog. She glanced back at him and wondered what he was thinking.

I must look like a real loser, she thought.

"You have a headache?"

"I do." She rubbed her head. "I got hit on the head, I guess."

"Are you dizzy? Is your vision blurry?" Doc asked.

"I was dizzy, but not now. It's just this headache."

He stood up. "Back in a sec," he said. He returned and handed her a glass of water and two aspirin.

She looked at him gratefully. "Thanks."

G.G. swallowed the aspirin and drank the

water. Then she settled back with her coffee.

Doc watched all this silently. He was tired from work. Rowing the big dog had just about done him in. He needed to sleep. He didn't want to bail out on a fellow Guy in need, but he was a tired tiger, unused to guests.

G.G. looked at the brandy bottle and held up her coffee cup. "Mind if I splash in a little more?"

"No, not at all. Help yourself."

G.G. got up and said, "You're probably wondering what's going on here."

"It did cross my mind."

"I'm captain of the *Sea Dog*, my fish boat, which seems to have been made off with."

"Your boat's gone? Stolen gone?"

"Seems to be." She sat back down and looked across at him. He looked worn out. She didn't feel any better than he looked. "What happened is, these two hired me for last night, to cruise along the piers, they said."

"Fog was pretty thick last night," Doc pointed out.

G.G. shrugged. "Yeah, it was. But they still wanted to go. After we'd been out about an hour, the big one, he says he wants me to take my skiff and row his partner under the pier at Murkey's."

"Murkey's!" Doc sat up.

"Yeah. 'No way,' I said. 'The tide's too high,

no clearance, stupid idea!'"

"Yeah, last night it was pretty high." He sipped his coffee. "But why under Murkey's?"

"They never said. In any case, I was not going to let some random Guy take command of my boat while I rowed off. No way! But he pulls out a gun and says, 'Think again.' So, me and the partner row off. As we leave, he says he'll be watching us. Through the rifle scope!" G.G. shook her head, remembering.

"So, we get to the pier; there's barely enough clearance, I'm leaning down so I don't hit my head, dodging the pilings, and a ship comes steaming in toward the estuary at a good clip. Her wake rolls in and catches us under the pier before I could row out. We're smacked up into the underside of the pier. My head got a good thump; knocked me out, I guess. No idea what happened after that."

"Well," said Doc, "You had a close call. You probably have a little concussion. You sure you're not dizzy?"

"No, not anymore." She felt behind her ear and winced again. "I do have a pretty good bump here."

"I can fix an ice pack, if you want."

"No, no. I've had enough cold already. These aspirin are kicking in."

There was silence while they both sipped coffee. G.G. looked at Doc.

"I must have been there for hours, I guess. I kept coming to and passing out." G.G. shivered again and moved closer to the heater. She took another swallow of the good, hot coffee. "Wow! I'm lucky you came along."

They sat in comfortable silence for a little while. The sailboat rocked gently and the heater glowed. Doc refilled their cups with more coffee and brandy. He sat back down and looked at the dog. Her eyes drooped half closed.

"You still haven't told me your name," he said.

G.G. shifted and looked into her coffee. "No, I guess I haven't." She shrugged. "I'm G.G., just a dog that's down on her luck." She stirred the coffee around.

Doc hesitated and then asked, "You got anywhere to go?"

She grimaced. "Well, now that you mention it, I don't, really." She looked around the small boat.

"Well," Doc said.

"I hate to beg, but if I could just get a couple hours of sleep here." The warm cabin was relaxing, and she didn't think she could stay awake much longer. "I know, I've got to call the Coast Guard about my boat, but at this point, what's the hurry? Right now, I can barely keep my eyes open."

She looked at Doc, her big black eyes pleading more than she intended.

"Maybe that's the best solution. I'm tired too. I just got off work. Let's catch some sleep and then see where we're at."

He got up. "This banquette slides open—you can sleep here. My berth's forward, and the head's just on the other side of the bulkhead. I'll see if I have an extra toothbrush."

"Maybe we'll hold the tooth brushing for later," G.G. said. She already had the banquette slid out. Doc handed a blanket and pillow to the exhausted dog. He rinsed the cups in the sink, stowed the brandy, and disappeared forward to his berth.

Soon the sailboat floated in silence.

8: A Place to Hide Out

After Moose slipped out of Murkey's, he did not tarry. Was he tired! At least he had one lucky break tonight: Bill the Bum still had his unofficial moose club on Sipp's Creek. If a moose needed a place to lie low, Bill was there for you.

Gotta get back ta Bill's. Be safer off the street. Get some sleep.

Keeping alert, he hoofed it down The Embarcadero. He went quick, yet to anyone out that late, he appeared completely unhurried.

Halfway across the Sipp's Creek bridge at Third Street he looked inland. Nothing rippled the surface of the old waterway. As far as he could tell, the creek was empty to the Fourth Street Bridge, barely visible through the fog. On the south side of the canal, he stepped off the pavement and onto a narrow footpath through the weeds. A little piece of him relaxed. Even if it was just a weedy path along this stubby little creek in the middle of the city, he always felt more grounded when he was off the concrete.

He passed the Fourth Street Bridge, paused under a meager tree and studied the houseboats ahead. A couple of them still had lights on. Bill's place was dark. But then, it always was. That's how Bill liked it. Completely low profile.

Moose looked around for the two crazy seagulls that kept watch on the creek. No reason to alarm them, wake the whole creek up. Right now, no seagulls could be seen. Earlier, they had shadowed him while he waited for Bill to open his door. Bill had said he'd let them know Moose was OK to pass any time.

He eased down the muddy slope to the floating ramp and was just about to step onto it when *fwip!* —a gull landed in front of him on the ramp. Was it Juke or Jake? He couldn't tell them apart. All doggone gulls looked alike. Whichever one it was, the gull gave him a sharp look.

Keeping his voice low, Moose said, "It's me. I'm going back ta Bill's."

The gull stood his ground for a moment and gave Moose a steely once-over. Slowly he moved to one side, barely leaving Moose enough room to slip by.

Moose could feel the gull behind him, watching him walk the whole way down the wobbling ramp. As he approached Bill's door, Moose glanced up and saw the other seagull perched above it. He looked back at the door as it silently opened. He eased into the darkened hallway.

Bill closed the door behind him without a click and flipped on the light. A very low light shone from the ceiling bulb and illuminated the hallway, not so narrow, but a tight fit for two moose. Bill motioned for Moose to go ahead of him. Still without a sound, they entered the kitchen. With the door to the kitchen closed, Bill finally spoke, keeping his voice soft.

"Moose. Ya hungry? I got rice and stew on the stove. Or I could whip ya up some eggs."

Moose sat down and stretched. "Ah, Bill. Good to see ya. I'm tired; not sure I could eat, thanks. Man, them seagulls ya got out there are good. I was lookin' fer 'em, but I couldn't see a feather of 'em 'til I stepped up ta the walkway."

Bill limped over and put two beers on the table. "Juke and Jake? Yeah. Those two. They been around. They get a little flaky now and then, but most of the time they're on it. Ya know seagulls: not much gets past any of 'em." He chuckled. "'Specially if there's food involved. So."

Bill took a slug of beer. "Haven't seen ya in how long! How ya doing there, Moose? Drink up!"

Moose M'Boy and Bill the Bum have a beer.

Moose sipped his beer. He didn't really like beer but he might as well be sociable. Bill was letting him stay there, after all.

"Bill, Bill. Ya old moth-eaten son of a mink coat. Ya lookin' good. What's keepin' ya outta trouble? The place is lookin' good here. Business good?"

"Can't complain. Ya seen all them antlers I keep up on the roof, ain't ya? The ones from

Guys have passed on, right? Well, sorry ta say, I added another pair last week."

"No kiddin'! Who died?"

"Remember M'n'M? Missouri Moose? Him. A Guy working with him brung 'em over ta me just two days ago. I had ta clean 'em up some—he had a' accident trying ta blow a safe."

Moose shook his head. "And him so careful alla time, too. Hard ta believe. Well, here's ta M'n'M!"

They held their beer bottles aloft and drank a solemn toast to the departed. "Well, Bill, if my antlers end up on yer roof, it'll be a' honor." He took another sip of beer. "Not many a' the old crowd left. Seen Towtruck lately?"

"He's been gone. Ain't heard where," said Bill. "Dropped off the map, maybe two-three years after ya went away." He glanced sideways toward his guest. "Lookin' fer him, are ya?"

"Nah, not really. Just wonderin', is all."

They drank their beers and talked a little longer, two old acquaintances sharing tales without giving away any useful information.

Moose's day had been long and tiring. The beer made him even sleepier. Before he could nod off at the table, Bill showed him a side room where he could rest undisturbed. That was all Moose knew for some time.

9: A Death in The Fog

So! It's now after 4 o'clock in the foggy morning of our story. Where is everybody right now? Doc has rescued G.G. and rowed her to his sailboat on Sipp's Creek. Moose has gone to ground at Bill's houseboat, also on Sipp's Creek. Webbs is home, fast asleep, and Bongo, the same. As for Ida and Hamms, they're busy finishing up the baking chores.

Where is Bunz? Out in the cold, dank air of the fish docks. Bongo has trotted off, and the rabbit is wondering if he should stall around and wait for Silver D. to show up at the Lodge Motel.

No—waste of time; he had no idea when Silver D. might show.

To shake off the chill, the rabbit started walking again. There is very little traffic along The Embarcadero so early in the day. Only ones out and about are delivery drivers and early-bird workers who prep the morning for the rest of the city: deckhands, ferry boat captains, cab drivers, bus and streetcar operators, and first-shift coffee shop crews.

The fish boats are already out to sea. The rest of the city sleeps.

The rabbit walked along, brooding. Were the moose sniffing around Murkey's or were they not? There had been no real whiff of a moose trail yet. As he approached Pier 41, Bunz thought again about talking to the gulls; Nosey Parker, nosiest of seagulls, had a nest nearby. It was early, but it couldn't hurt to see if Nose was up.

Bunz turned off the sidewalk and angled over to the floating docks at the ferry terminal. Four ferryboats were tied up, and their crews worked to get them ready for the day: filling fresh water tanks, hosing the boats down, pumping out sewage tanks, checking fuel levels, stopping for a quick chat.

With all this action, how could Nosey not be awake?

As Bunz stood there, a seagull swooped down and landed beside him. Nosey Parker, right on schedule. And, always ready to eat, the gull had his fork with him. This lightened the rabbit's mood. If Nosey was hungry, he would be willing to deal. He favored the bird with a small smile.

"Mornin', Nose."

"Mornin', B. What's got you out so early? Had breakfast?"

"Nosey Parker. Just the gull I want to 'sea'.

Ha-ha!" Bunz snorted at his cheesy joke.

Nosey surveyed the rabbit. Always the wiseacre. Not that you'd mention it to him.

Bunz continued unabashed, "You know anything about a large moose been seen around here the last few days? With a little sidekick that smiles a lot?"

"Two moose?"

Bunz made no reply but thought, *Isn't that what I just said?* He looked steadily at the bird. Nosey stared back. *He's got something,* thought Bunz, *or he wouldn't be asking dumb questions.*

Into the salty silence Bunz finally answered. "Yes. Two moose."

"Yesterday."

"Think they're locals?" asked Bunz.

"No."

Bunz sighed, irked at the short answers. This was like pulling teeth, only birds didn't have teeth. *Ha-ha,* he chuckled. "And? You noticed them. Why?"

"They stuck out, you know."

"You saw two moose and they stuck out," Bunz said dryly. "Not a big crowd of moose tourists that day?"

"All dressed up they were, but cheap suits, flashy, from like ten years ago."

Bunz kept his expression flat. "And?"

"One of them smiled too much."

"What else?"

"Nothing."

"Nothing? Joe Maartuni saw them asking questions."

"So go ask Joe."

"Already did. Now I'm asking you."

Nosey looked at the rabbit. *Short-fuse rabbit,* the gull thought. *He really wants something. Wonder what.* The gull waited to see what Bunz would do next.

"What time did you see them?"

"Can't really say. Was this family left a mess of food behind, so I—"

"It was around lunchtime?"

"No, see—"

Bunz heaved a weary sigh. "I don't want your entire day, Nose. Just tell me about the moose."

Nosey shook his feathers and harrumphed. It was too early for this wisenheimer rabbit, and besides, he was hungry.

Bunz gave Nosey's fork a glance. "Had breakfast?"

That got Nosey's attention.

"No."

Bunz waited.

"First saw them late morning. OK?"

"You know you always get something from me if your information is good."

"Saw them again later. Want to know where?"

"Try me."

"First time was here, studying ferry schedules. Later, they were near Castoffola's, talking to Captain G.G."

Bunz said nothing and let the pause linger.

Nosey added, "They wanted a charter. For last night."

"In all this fog?"

"Was it foggy in the afternoon?" the bird asked acidly.

Bunz frowned. "No."

"Anyway, I happen to know that G.G. needs work. Some of us gulls had a business arrangement with—"

Bunz cut him off. "Did they go out with this G.G. last night?"

"Maybe." Nosey narrowed his eyes. In fact, he didn't know. He shuffled his feet. "Come on, Bunz. I don't spend my days snooping around for free."

"Hey. Look, Nose. This is good stuff. Just tell me, what's the name of his boat?"

"Her boat."

"OK. Her boat."

"The *Sea Dog*."

"The *Sea Dog*, near Castoffola's. And did they go out last night?"

"Go ask G.G.!" *Why was the rabbit so interested in two moose?*

The seagull was almost curious, but first

things first. It was past his breakfast time. He picked up his fork and turned to leave.

"You might be interested," Bunz said.

The bird paused in his crouch for takeoff.

"I was at Murkey's earlier," Bunz added.

Nosey loved Murkey's. He gave his full attention to Bunz.

"They had two-day-old pastries. They don't sell the two-day stuff. You might—"

Before Bunz could finish, Nosey sprang into the air and flew off.

A muffled "Thanks, B!" swirled back in the draft beneath his wings.

Bunz grinned as the gull disappeared. Nosey didn't realize it, but he'd given away something valuable. Two Guys wearing loud, out-of-date suits just might have been living at the expense of the state and been released recently. Could be that the moose were straight-up real crooks, not miserable real estate promoters.

What would crooks want with Murkey's? Maybe this Captain G.G. can give me their names.

Bunz veered back toward the fish docks and Castoffola's. A few fish boats—the ones that hired out to tourists—were tied up alongside the sidewalk. As he moseyed along checking boat names, he thought, *Police records will show what these two were into. I'll get the*

*names from this G.G., drop by the old precinct
and get Den to check a few things out.*

He reached the last boat in the row but
there was no *Sea Dog*. One empty slip held a
place near the middle of the row of boats. If
it belonged to the *Sea Dog*, she was not back
from her evening trip. Charter boats don't
go out till daybreak at the earliest, so where
was the *Sea Dog*? Too early to find anyone to
question.

The rabbit turned back to the south. Morning
traffic was starting to build. An early runner
passed him, feet slapping the damp concrete.
A fleet of brimming trucks had parked near
Pier 27, their contents being off-loaded, ready
to be stowed in the glossy cruise ship that
was due in. Out in the deep-water channel,
a towering container ship plowed through
the water, dwarfing the massive pier shed
as she passed. Her fog signal moaned as she
headed toward the Bay Bridge and the Port of
Oakland.

The rabbit figured, *If I can see that ship, the
fog's starting to lift.*

The bow of the huge ship threw off a wake
that curled toward shore. Fifty feet from The
Embarcadero, a large timber swayed with the
tide. In the wake's passing undulation, the
sodden timber see-sawed. A gull, balanced on
top of it, calmly compensating for the flow of

the wave. The little wave sauntered onward and rolled under the pier. If you stood close, you could hear the *shhhhh shhhhh* as it collapsed against the riprap at the foot of The Embarcadero seawall.

A Coast Guard patrol boat fled past. B.'s eye followed the blinking blue light on the fast little craft as it headed in the same direction he was going.

Are they rushing to an incident or just burning through fuel?

At Pier 13 he decided to check in at the diner. Webbs might still be there—that could happen. When the spider fixated on a problem, he lost all track of time. Bunz glanced in the diner window. No black, fuzzy spider. Disappointed, he turned away and shoved his paws deeper in his pockets.

At the pier south of Murkey's, red, flashing lights caught his eye. A fire truck was at the curb in front of Pier 9, but he saw no smoke. Curious, he walked over to investigate. In the open water between Pier 11 and Pier 9, the little Coast Guard boat had stopped, blue lights still flashing. A city fireboat and a wooden rowboat were clustered together. The fire truck crew looked on from the dock.

The Guy in the rowboat was pointing. Under Pier 9, a small body floated in the water, face down. It shifted gently in the water, bumped against a dark piling. A breeze shivered by. Someone on deck of the Coast Guard boat called across to the fireboat crew, but the breeze stole their voices away before Bunz could hear what they said.

The fireboat maneuvered close in to the body. A crew member deployed a long boat hook over the side and began the grim task of pulling the soggy remains from the water. Two other crew members reached down and hoisted the body up over the side of the boat. Wet brown fur dripped onto the deck. They laid the body gently down and stepped back.

Bunz caught sight of a small pair of antlers. *Another moose, or one of the same two?*

Swooping out of the fog, a seagull circled over the boats and then wheeled toward Bunz. The breeze of wings ruffled the rabbit's fur as Nosey Parker landed near him. His gullet bulged with his recent breakfast.

Looks like he ate pretty good, Bunz thought.

Nosey sidled over and said, "You're not going to believe this, Bunz."

"Believe what?"

"Guess who that is."

"A moose who wanted a boat ride?"

"Yup. The one with the neon smile."

"Not smiling now."

They gazed at the sodden carcass on the deck of the fireboat.

Still looking at the corpse, Bunz said, "The way the tides were last night, that moose could have washed in from anywhere, or just floated around under this pier all night. What slip does that G.G. tie her boat up at?"

"Kinda in the middle, along the sidewalk."

"Well, I just came from there. Only one empty slip. And no *Sea Dog*."

Nosey eyed B. "Gotta be G.G.'s slip then." He looked back at the dead moose.

"Think they would have stayed out all night?"

"Unlikely," said Nosey.

The two Guys watched the three boats negotiate the narrow space between piers. Gradually their attention was drawn to an object scraping around between the pilings under Pier 11. It appeared to be a half-sunk wooden skiff.

Suddenly, Nosey rocked forward and stared. "I'm for sure that's G.G.'s skiff! Why is it here? Where the heck is her fish boat?"

"A fish boat's kinda big to lose," Bunz drawled.

Nosey looked at the rabbit. He had just flashed on an angle he might turn to his favor. "You know what? Her slip is only a ten-minute flight from here. I'm going to check. Maybe she's back now."

Bunz held back a smile. The Nose was

back on patrol. "OK. Let me know if you find it or not. I'll go bother Doc. Maybe he saw something on his row home."

"Yeah, he could have." Nosey crouched for take-off and added, "If G.G.'s not back at her berth, I'll cruise the bay, ask around. Check with you later."

With a crisp flap of wings, he launched himself into the air, pivoted north and disappeared back into the fog.

Bunz stayed and watched the three boats. After some palaver, they all left. The fire truck rolled off. Bunz was alone.

He still had no answers. But there were a few new questions. Where was the *Sea Dog*? How did this moose get dead? And where was the other moose?

He started walking again, toward the ballpark and Sipp's Creek.

10: Sipp's Creek

Once it had been a beautiful, living creek. The waters of the ancient creek flowed down from the coastal highlands, carrying fresh water to the Native American inhabitants and to the bay. The Spanish immigrants that came to the area in the mid-1800's named the bay Estero de la Mision. When the Americans showed up, the creek became Mission Creek. It was the original source of pure water for the settlement built beside the bay, and was celebrated in song and verse for its beauty.

Not any longer. What happened? First, it was thoroughly polluted. Then they built the railroad over it, and then the freeway.

During Gold Rush times, Mission Bay and Mission Creek were busy shipping links. The waterfront south of Market Street was filled with ships and smoke and noise, business and factories of all sorts. Ships came and went from crowded docks built along Mission Bay and along the creek banks. Small boats sailed for pleasure up Mission Creek.

New docks were built further north, closer

to the Golden Gate. The creek saw the relocation of the dynamic shipping business to the new docks and the resulting demise of the old shipyards and smoking iron works.

Then came the landfill craze. The landfill gimmick was implemented with the mercenary idea of 'water lots.' The great Mission Bay tidal basin was surveyed and these 'water lots' were laid out across it, declared legal by the city and sold off. Eager land promoters filled in their water lots with rotting ship timbers and any other thing available, the cheaper the better. The new 'land' was then resold at a good profit.

Mission Bay, the lagoon, ceased to exist and became Mission Bay, the neighborhood—manmade real estate barely above the water table. Through those years of destruction and transformation, a few hundred yards of the prehistoric creek managed to elude the landfill frenzy.

The city grew large as it plundered California of her riches, and this watery relic is the last testimony of the primeval creek. To see the waters as they once were, you must search out old paintings and photographs.

Even today, short-sighted developers build on the bones of the old bay, despite predictions that low-lying landfill will flood as sea levels rise, and will likely liquify during an earthquake. The latest ventures: a baseball stadium and a flossy new hospital, built so the latest tycoon can plaster his name around the city.

Now in the shadow of freeway overpasses, this remaining stub of the creek flows between concrete banks to the bay. It is still crossed by the sturdy iron bridges that endure from that long-gone shipping era. And the creek cumulated enough history to earn itself a nickname: Sipp's Creek.

Sipp's Creek: a nickname derived from a bad reputation. During the first Prohibition, the aging wharves and abandoned warehouses were repurposed into drinking dens frequented by thirsty customers looking for a good time. For a brief period, the creek was 'in the money' again, as drinkers flocked there to get a 'sip' at illicit speakeasies.

At the big hotels and high-toned restaurants, there was plenty of black-market liquor, but wasn't it more fun to go down to Sipp's! And naturally, it was these two-bit joints along the canal that got raided, not the fancy hotels. The joints were closed; the ramshackle buildings were condemned. The old wharves sank further into the deserted creek. Commerce moved on.

When a few scalawag houseboats began to populate the old canal, no one was there to take notice. The waterway became home to a patchwork of houseboats and sailboats, and a few birds. Guys who couldn't make it anywhere else hung on here and scraped out a living.

Then came the Sugar Ban. The canal saw new action. Some Guys turned their houseboats into Sugar Shacks, all-night joints where you could get a soda pop smuggled in from out-of-state, and sweets made with real sugar. Other houseboats concealed cutting rooms, where the sugar was cut with rice flour or corn starch, and street dealers loaded up with small bags to sell for big bucks. Even now, ten years later, it was a sound bet that some of Doc's neighbors operated on the far side of the law.

Yet and still, in spite of the disrepair and the looming freeway, there was a bucolic feel to the little neighborhood. A walk along its banks hearkened back to pastoral times. Grasses and trees thrived here and there. A pair of ducks nested. If you were patient and lucky, you might glimpse an occasional fish in the dense water.

It is true that creek dwellers embraced capricious hours. But there is that time of day when even those who stay up late are slumbering and the creek is quiet. But tonight, there was one rabbit awake. He lurked on the heavy old bascule bridge that crossed the creek at Fourth Street, out of sight behind the bridge superstructure.

The creek had not changed much since his Pie Inspector days. The rickety, floating walkways still connected the houseboats to each other and to the muddy shore. The pieced-together houseboats were shabbier than he remembered. He studied the sailboats tied up here and there. Which one was Doc's?

Well, thought Bunz, *I do know his rowboat. It's a cinch he ties up near his sailboat.*

But he couldn't see the rowboat from the bridge. He would have to get closer. Two seagulls mucked about in the shallows, looking for food. He knew they were not merely eating an early breakfast. They had a sharp eye out for interlopers.

He thought about that. Get close enough to the gulls to deal with them quietly.

A breeze ruffled the rabbit's fur. *Time to move. Just have to drift by slow, hope neither of them recognizes me. If we tangle,* he thought, *they'll get the whole canal in an uproar. Doc will put me in the deep freeze, I'll get nothing.*

He crossed the bridge and made his way along the crude shore path, gaping like he'd never been to the creek before.

Imperceptibly, the two guard gulls turned their attention to the intruder.

Bunz kept one eye on the gulls, and one eye out for Doc's blue skiff. Houseboat, houseboat, sailboat, no blue skiff. At one houseboat, Bunz stopped to stare. A collection of dried-out antlers had been nailed to its sides and piled on the flat of the roof.

Morbid. Very weird. Don't remember those being here ten years ago.

He strolled on. Nothing. Nothing. Nothing. He was nearing the last houseboat. No blue skiff came into view. The gulls were getting tense.

If only Nosey were here. From the air, Nosey could easily spot Doc's skiff.

The rabbit looked at the sky.

Should I wait for him? Heck no—that gull might not land here for hours.

One more step, and he saw it—the little blue skiff. Tied to the floating walkway, just like he figured. At the far side of a truly dilapidated houseboat, he saw the stern of a sailboat protruding. Looked like a good-size boat for a small tiger!

The rabbit angled down the bank and stepped onto the wooden span that connected the floating walkway to shore. As the span took his weight, it waggled a little too forcefully. He paused to let it settle. The two seagulls had seen enough. They paddled over, their beady eyes clearly focused on him.

Here we go, he thought.

He hopped back to shore and waved as he went toward the gulls. "Hi, Guys." He tried a smile.

The gulls stood silent in the shallows, wing to wing, and gave him a hard look.

"You two are up early."

They didn't appear to recognize him. They stood unmoving, and demonstrated their double stony stare.

"You live around here?"

Hostile restraint from the gulls.

"Perhaps you can help me. I'm a friend of Doc's, but I don't know which boat he lives on."

Bunz paused. Finally, one gull spoke up.

"Doc who?"

"Doc who works at Murkey's. I know him from Murkey's."

"Murkey's, huh? If you're a friend, how come you don't know his boat, huh?"

"Never been to his boat."

"Maybe he don't want you on his boat. Think of that, did ya?"

The gull not talking looked off. He was done with this dialog.

"That's his skiff." Bunz pointed to the blue boat.

A blast of silence from both gulls.

How do I get around these pinfeather heads?

He looked past the gulls and saw the antler houseboat. It gave him an idea. *Maybe I can interest them in a dead moose story.*

He eyed the gulls. "I s'pose you heard about the dead moose."

"Dead moose?" said the talky gull. "Dead moose where?"

Now he had their attention. "I'm thinking Doc maybe saw something on his row home today."

"Maybe saw what?"

"Don't know." Bunz made a show of scanning the sky. "Thought Nosey would be here by now."

The two birds looked at each other.

The talky gull said, "Nosey? Nosey Parker?"

Bunz put some surprise in his voice. "You know Nosey? He was there. He saw it." Casually he added, "It was Nosey who suggested maybe Doc saw something."

The two birds exchanged a glance. The silent gull shook his head 'No' and made a show of looking across the creek, along the bank, anywhere but at the rabbit.

But the talky one couldn't resist. "Nosey, huh?"

"Yeah." Bunz leaned back and eyed the gulls. "We agreed to meet up here after he ate."

"Well."

The talky gull stared at Bunz, and then he

cocked his head and looked at his partner.

Jake shook his head again and growled, "No, Juke."

"How about I just wait here till Nosey arrives. We can see Doc together."

Bunz looked placidly at Jake's angry scowl. *Gotcha! Don't want the neighborhood seeing a stranger hanging around, huh?*

Juke couldn't hold back. *Why not see what Doc says? Ol' Jake's too conservative. Something's going on. And we'll see if Nosey shows up.*

He shuffled his wings and turned to the rabbit. "I'll go talk to Doc."

Jake eyed Juke furiously.

Juke continued, "See if he's up. Bet he's sleeping though." He gave Bunz a flat look. "You wait here." The gull took off, circled the disintegrating houseboat and disappeared behind it.

Furious, the silent gull turned his beady eye on Bunz. A pair of ducks glided past—at a distance. No reason to get too close. Gull business was never their business.

Juke appeared on the roof of the old houseboat and waved a wing. The silent gull looked at Bunz and jerked his beak toward the walkway.

"What's the matter? Tiger got your tongue?" Bunz asked.

In a raspy voice, the gull replied, "When I got something to say, I say it. For you I got nothing." He turned and led the way down the floating walkway.

Ha! Who cares? Bunz held back a grin and stepped onto the walkway. At the sailboat, they stopped. Juke skimmed down, landing next to them.

"Doc says give him a minute."

Nearby, Doc's blue skiff bumped against the walkway. A tired tiger appeared on the deck of the sailboat. Looking at Doc, Bunz realized that he'd had a long night himself. He gave Doc a nod.

"Morning, Doc!" Steadying himself against the boat hull, he started to climb aboard.

Doc waved him off and said, "No, no, don't bother. I'll come down."

Bunz felt a flash of irritation. He didn't want to go through his whole story in front of the gulls. He stepped back as the tiger jumped lightly onto the walkway. It barely moved as he landed.

Bunz gave Doc a pointed look. He cocked his head toward the sailboat and waited. Doc ignored the hint.

Cussed gulls! Bunz thought. He turned his back to the gulls and lowered his voice. "See anything on your row home today?"

Doc squinted closely at the rabbit. "Why do you ask?"

Bunz hesitated. He felt the gulls staring at him behind his back.

"Anything like what?" Doc added.

"Like a drowned moose was found this morning."

Doc's whiskers flared as he digested the news. "Dead?"

"All the way dead. You saw nothing?"

The tiger growled, "No dead bodies, if that's what you're asking."

"Nothing unusual?"

Doc scowled. "Who was the dead Guy?"

The gulls leaned closer, hungry for details. Bunz stalled.

"Oh, alright. Come on aboard, then." He turned toward his boat. Over his shoulder he said to the seagulls, "You Guys keep up the good work."

"Yeah, thanks Guys!" Bunz said, grinning. He followed the tiger aboard. They went below to a neat little cabin. Bunz stared at the most prominent feature.

"I didn't know you had a dog." He moved over to the heater and turned to Doc, who was busy making coffee at the stove.

Doc said, "Not my dog. I picked her up on my way home tonight. You may or may not be surprised to know that's G.G., captain of the fish boat *Sea Dog*."

"Really!" Bunz sat down on the portside

banquette opposite the dog. "Tell me."

Doc handed a mug of coffee to the rabbit and sat down next to him. The big dog did not stir as they drank their coffee and Doc filled Bunz in on his adventure.

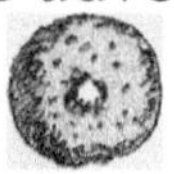

"Well," said Bunz. He set his empty mug down on the banquette beside him. "Lucky for her, she didn't get swept out to sea."

"Yeah. Or worse." Doc took the empty mugs. "So. The Nose is off looking for the *Sea Dog*?" He poured more coffee and glanced at the sleeping dog. "She'll be glad to hear that. I don't think she has anywhere to go except that boat."

He handed the rabbit fresh coffee and leaned back. "Guests aren't my thing. But I couldn't kick her out after what she went through." He pointed to the heater. "Is it too hot in here for you? I could turn it down."

"Feels good to me."

"Little too warm for me," said the tiger. "But she was about frozen stiff, and soaking wet."

Bunz looked at the dog sleeping under a warm blanket. "You've got that thicker fur, Doc," he said. "And there's nothing like being cold and wet to take it out of you."

They were silent for a moment, thinking how one mistake on the water can go so bad, so fast.

Bunz said, "Saw a little screwed up skiff smacking around under Pier 11. Hers, huh?"

"It's still there?" said Doc. "She didn't seem to think it would be worth fixing. But I don't know. Nice old wooden skiff, might be worth a look, if it's there later." He yawned. "Wonder if the Nose found anything."

"I told him I was headed here," said B. "If he finds out anything, he'll probably stop by. Lucky for me those two gulls you got out there know him. Otherwise I don't think I would have gotten past them."

He chuckled.

Doc did not. "Yeah, well." Doc reached over to turn down the heater. The less Bunz asked about living on the creek, the better. "They're good Guys."

Bunz sensed the watchfulness in Doc, something he knew to expect from those living on Sipp's Creek. He looked around the cabin and wondered how Doc had ended up living here. This boat he lived on—outside it looked like a Loser's Creek special, but inside it was cozy and ship-shape. The tiger had been a cook at Murkey's a few years now. Liked the late shift. Once he had let drop that he had been a medic in the war. And here he was, helping out the dog, letting her stay over, even though he preferred not to.

More to this Guy than meets the eye, Bunz

thought. He looked at G.G. *And what about this dog? Could be she's in on the moose scheme.* "That story she told you. Do you believe it?" Bunz asked.

"I don't know." Doc was silent for a few moments. "It's curious that the moose walked into the diner a few hours after stealing her boat."

"I'd say he's in a hurry about something."

"And Ida said he asked about the trap door."

"Did he? Another way to get under Murkey's then."

"Yep. But only thing under there is that old retractable stair."

Bunz laughed. "The Smuggler's Friend? That still there? Tide was so high earlier, it was covered up. Maybe I'll go over later and give it a look-see."

"Nothing left but rust."

Bunz mulled over the dog's story. G.G. lay still, snoring softly. *There's a joke in there somewhere,* Bunz thought. *Are sleeping dogs lying or not?* But he was tired and couldn't figure out how to make it funny.

"Did the dog mention any names?"

"Didn't ask."

The rabbit stretched and waggled his feet. "We'll have a little chat when she wakes up." *And see how she tells me the story.*

Doc made no reply. The silence lengthened. The tiger looked over to see the rabbit's eyes closed. *Geez. Suddenly my boat is a hotel.* He collected the cups, rinsed them in the sink, and went forward to his sleeping quarters in the bow.

Houseboats on Sipp's Creek—
the last of the once-beautiful Mission Creek.

11: Webbs Awakens

Donuts on the offensive! Attack donuts of every flavor storming into the bay!

Webbs crouches down and peeks out the diner window. Giant donuts flood in with the tide! Attack donuts bigger than boats roll toward the pier and pitch themselves against it! Jelly donuts! Glazed donuts! Maple bars! The bay is infested with them! They swarm around the diner and smack against the pilings. The old pier quakes; the pilings creak and tremble. Oh, no! A weak spot! Crazy loud banging as the donuts assail the hatch and pound against it from below!

The hatch cover is loose! Up and down it bangs against the kitchen floor boards. The battered old lock begins to give way. The weight of giant donuts on the old hardware is too much! POW! The lock shears apart! Jagged pieces of metal fly across the kitchen. Ping! Dong! The pots chime as they are hit. The hatch cover pops up with the pressure of invading donuts. Jelly-filled! Chocolate! Crullers!

Webbs cringes back. Oh, no! Run, Spide! Run!

Webbs jerked awake. Stunned, he lay under the covers and stared at the ceiling. *Giant donuts? Ack! What a terrible dream. Why am I dreaming about attack donuts? Banging against that old hatch cover. Crushing the pier? Wow. Too weird for wingnuts.*

He shook his head and let the blankness of the ceiling calm his mind. Cozy under the covers, he looked around his little one-room place high on the hill.

Webbs wakes up from a bad donut dream.

It might be small, but how much room

did one spider need? Large windows faced south, letting light in all day. This he liked. Even on foggy days his place was still bright. The kitchen was small and practical. He had room for his books, a good reading chair, a worktable, and his little electric piano. At night, he hung his hammock on two hooks and was happy as any spider in a web. How lucky he was to have rent control, too. Otherwise, he would have been forced to move out years ago.

His thoughts wandered. That floor hatch—it fascinated anyone who heard about it, thanks to the smuggling tales.

Old crimes were so romantic. He did love listening to the old-timers tell flamboyant yarns about the wild days and nights on the waterfront. The characters that hung around the wharves back then! The longshore Guys, the sailors from around the world, the lunatics who operated the railroad that had run along the waterfront. The clever rumrunners, and the treacherous types bootlegging sugar from not so long ago.

Some of those stories were true, but which ones? He loved ferreting out the truth, and wondered: had liquor really been smuggled in through Murkey's? Gran'dad never would say directly, but some of Webbs' other sources said yes.

The spider sniffed with a hint of smugness. A real sleuth never believed rumors—he always checked his facts. How had the sequence of smuggling worked? If steamships brought the booze down from Canada, and motor launches and fish boats sneaked the stuff into the bay— did someone just row under Murkey's, knock on the hatch cover and sell a few bottles to the kitchen crew? Or was Murkey's part of a distribution chain, and whole crates of whiskey were hauled up through the hatch and out the back door into trucks that carried it off the pier for distribution?

What about the bootleg sugar—it was kind of an open secret that the bakers at Murkey's had used the real stuff during the sugar ban. Was Murkey's also a drop and distribution center for big sugar shipments?

How bootleg sugar moved around the city— now that would be a fun research project. Webbs stretched long and slow. Sometimes the best part of getting up was lying in bed and thinking about it. He snuggled further under the covers.

Just a few more minutes, then I'll get up.

The hammock swayed gently as he considered the day ahead.

Bunz thinks I daydream all the time, but I don't! I'm thinking. I'm going to find out who these moose are and what they're really up to. Why not try to figure out what's going and save Murkey's? If I can.

His stomach growled. A giant jelly donut floated into his consciousness. Ack! Definitely time to get up. He threw off the covers and jumped down, shivering in the cool air as he unhooked his hammock and stowed it away.

Time to get going with this research! He looked at the clock. Later than he thought. No time for a trip to Murkey's this morning.

Darn. Too bad one of those dream donuts isn't real, though it might go stale before I could eat it all! I wish I'd brought home a donut last night.

He chuckled as he wondered where he could store such a big donut in his little place. He turned on the oven to get a little heat in the air, grabbed the coffee, ground some beans, spooned the grounds into the little basket, and set his two-piece coffee maker on the stove. While he waited, he sat down at his worktable, picked up a pencil, and opened a notebook. Time for a list of research ideas.

It's funny. Everyone's all worried about those moose. I keep thinking about the old days and the stories Gran'dad told me. Something Bunz said got me started on that.

The notebook lay empty. He stared at the blank page and shook his head. The coffee maker burbled. He got up, turned off the flame, and poured a cup. The steam rose from the cup as he leaned over and sniffed it.

Ahhh, the great aroma of fresh coffee! He sat back in his chair and took another sniff: too hot to drink. He gazed out the window at the treetops. They looked less blurry. The fog was beginning to burn off with the promise of a beautiful day. He glanced at the empty notebook. It was time to get down to business.

He picked up the pencil. What were the different strands of this thing? On one side of the page he wrote 'Murkey's' and on the other, 'Moose.'

If the moose want to buy Murkey's, the connection lies between them and Sprinkhels. They'd buy the lease from Sprinkhels.

He erased 'Murkey's' and wrote 'Sprinkhels'. Under 'Sprinkhels' he wrote 'Lease.'

He doodled a dashed line between 'Moose' and 'Sprinkhels.' In the middle of the page above the dashed line, he wrote 'Murkey's.' He drew a box around 'Murkey's'. On top of the box, he doodled a little roof shingled in donuts.

He leaned back, sipped his coffee, and stared at the pad. A thought snagged at the back of his brain. What did Bunz say last night—something about the Sprinkhels clan.

He doodled some dollar bills on the dashes between 'Moose' and 'Sprinkhels.' He filled in the dollar doodles with little coins. Suddenly he remembered. They had been talking about the Sprinkhels' fortune and Bunz said, "They didn't get rich by turning down money."

So then, why did Sprinkhels Junior hold onto Murkey's? That was the puzzle. With Murkey's great location and the waterfront getting so popular, Junior must have had offers on the place, maybe big offers.

But he didn't sell. Why not?

Plus, if the diner wasn't on the market, all the local real estate Guys would know that. Strangers like these two moose would find out pretty quick, if they made legitimate inquiries.

So then, let's say they're not trying to buy the place. Why else would they be nosing around? I mean, who are these Guys?

His fur prickled. He remembered something Gran'dad often said: sooner or later all the kooks end up down at the wharf.

Something about this was kooky.

He picked up his cup and sipped.

Just a minute, Spide. Never mind who the moose are. Stay with Murkey's. There's something about Murkey's that's got those moose asking questions. Let's assume that Sprinkhels Junior isn't selling—and that he has good reason. What kind of secrets might the old diner hold?

Webbs tapped his pencil against the table

edge. Secrets? Hah! There were secrets all up and down the waterfront. The two prohibitions saw plenty of black-market action: dirty money, swindles, unsolved murders, deals going right and wrong every night. Guys who had been there told stories about cover-ups, double-crosses, rip-offs, and pay-offs. Where to begin?

Tap! Tap! Tap! went the pencil. The whiskey prohibition was probably too long ago to be in play now—but the sugar ban, not so much!

Bunz could give me stuff about the smuggling side of things. But for him, it's all dusty old history by now.

The spider sighed and gazed at the window, but his mind focused inward. *The Port leases might play a part. But the smuggling, the dirty money—if I can find a definite lead on that side of things, I might get Bunz thinking my way. If there is some sort of Murkey's secret, and it's big enough, maybe I can find a hint. What I need is history uncensored!*

And he would find that at the History Room at the Main Library: old precinct bulletins, neighborhood newsletters with the local crimes of the week, old phone books; maybe a newspaper columnist had hung out with the gangsters and pols, then wrote a memoir about the dirty old days. Microfiche archived old newspapers—maybe he could dig up a report on something printed in the morning edition that got spiked by the afternoon.

This would be fun! And, big bonus: his friend Marilyn, the librarian, was working today. She would love to help dig. He finished his coffee and set the cup in the sink. He grabbed his hat and his notebook, and shut the door behind him.

12: Nosey Shows Up

As the morning unfurled, the Sipp's Creek locals slept on, secure in the knowledge that Juke and Jake had their sharp eyes peeled. And indeed they did! The two guard gulls were not a bit sleepy! There was action afoot and they were itching to know more!

Bill the Bum with one of his shifty visitors. A dead moose found floating in the bay! And most startling, Doc had visitors on his boat! Not just one, but two! Never since that tiger had been on the creek had anyone been invited aboard his boat. What could be next?

Joggers passed. Morning traffic on the bridges swelled and slacked off. Two ducks swam by. At mid-morning, the fog burned off and the sun started its day of work. A heron flew in, perched on passing flotsam, and held her wings out to dry.

Late in the morning, the two guard gulls poked along the canal bank looking for snacks and waiting for developments. From the direction of the bay, a seagull cruised slowly above the creek. Jake caught Juke's eye and cocked his head. The two gulls watched the visitor coast slowly along the still water. They tracked his slow arc as he scrutinized the houseboats, and his coast down as he landed softly, right next to Doc's little blue rowboat.

Nosey folded his wings and shook his feathers down. He saw the hard-bitten pair advancing in formation toward him.

Nosey thought, *Whoa, these two flakes. Haven't seen these two in a crooked cod's age!*

"Juke! Jake!" he said. "You old sons of a rusty razor clam!"

Juke spread his wings in mock astonishment. "Hey now, Jake! Look at this! It's the ol' Nose."

Jake drilled the visitor with his most caustic look. Juke leaned toward Nosey with a probing eye and a taunting smile.

Nosey squared his stance and shot back, "Well, well. Guess you two didn't have to leave town after all. This been your palace since the earthquake then?"

"Gull's gotta live somewheres," said Juke, giving Nosey a sour smirk.

"The Creek keeps you busy?"

"We're Security," Juke retorted, gesturing with his beak. "Private. For the owners here."

Nosey quelled a smile, thinking: *These two on security. That's hilarious. Bet they gave Bunz a hard time. Sorry I missed that!*

The gulls eyeballed each other. Finally

Juke asked, "Old stomping grounds about the same?"

"Yeah," said Nosey. "About the same." He thought, *Actually, they're better since you two vamoosed.* He glanced over at Doc's skiff.

Juke followed the glance. *Gotta be he's looking for Doc's sailboat, too. And that rabbit.* "So, then. What brings you here?"

"Looking for a Guy." Neither Juke nor Jake replied. After a pause he added, "He came to see Doc early this morning."

The hard eyes of the two gulls raked over him. This was their turf. They were giving up nothing.

Nosey stifled his aggravation and said, "Maybe you two were still asleep, huh? Didn't see a rabbit today?"

Insulted, Juke spoke up. "There was a Guy. Claimed to know you. Long ears."

"Sounds like Bunz."

Jake blew out a hard snort. He rasped, "Bunz? Pie Inspector Bunz?"

Juke winced. *Bloody idiot—I shouldn't a let that stumpy rabbit pass.*

Nosey couldn't help chuckling at the reaction. "Used to be. He still here?"

"What's a cop doing here?" Jake demanded. His eyes flickered toward Doc's sailboat. Was Doc into something shady and they had missed it?

"Ex-cop." Nosey followed Juke's glance. "That Doc's sailboat?"

Jake said, "If he's not a cop, then why's he here?"

"He still at Doc's?"

Juke looked back at Doc's boat. "I'll let him know you're here." Deliberately he stepped in front of the visiting gull and crouched for takeoff.

In a blur of feathers, Nosey launched himself straight over Juke's head, calling back, "He knows me."

Juke ducked to avoid the rocketing gull and caught the peeved look in his partner's eye.

Jake snarled, "Like I said. Shoulda stopped that rabbit."

"Yeah," Juke said uneasily. Cheering up, he said, "It was Doc let him in, not us. We warned him. And maybe they'll be gone before anyone here wakes up."

As Nosey glided down to the sailboat, he saw a name painted across the stern in flowing script. The gilded paint was so faded and chipped that only an "M" and a "P" could be discerned, the beginning letters of two words that had long since flaked off.

His feet made a quiet little *fwip* sound landing on the aft deck. The wooden deck was worn but felt solid beneath his feet. He fwipped over to the hatch cover and listened.

Silence.

He was just about to knock when the hatch slid open. He was beak to whiskers with Doc. A grumpy Doc.

"What's all this noise out here?" Doc grouched.

"Did I wake you, Doc?"

"You and the rest of the world," Doc growled.

"Well, we got a situation here."

"Bunz filled me in," Doc grumped. He turned to go back into the cabin. "I got news for you. That fish boat captain? She's here." The tiger started down the ladder steps.

Nosey dropped his beak open in surprise. "G.G.'s here?"

"Yep. Come on below. Just remember: no poop on my boat."

Nosey ignored the rude remark and paused at the hatch to inspect the cabin. He hated the indoors—the air was always stuffy, and worse, no room to spread his wings. A heater was giving off too much heat, and the small cabin was overfull with one large dog, the rabbit, and Doc. Rabbit and dog: sleeping. Bunz sprawled sideways on one banquette and G.G. was just now stirring under a blanket on the other.

Doc was at work in the little galley tucked in starboard side, alongside the ladder. A large pot of coffee was working, and Doc was slicing ripe mango onto a plate laden with pastries. Perched where he was, the gull was close at hand to the galley counter and still in the fresh air. He hopped down one step, still outside, but that much closer to the food. He waited impatiently for Doc to finish arranging fruit slices.

Nosey's stomach let out a growl. Breakfast had been a long time ago. *Ah! Which pastry was biggest: the apricot Danish or the cherry Danish?*

Awakened by voices, Bunz opened one eye. Was that Doc making more coffee? Hadn't he just made coffee? The rabbit squinted at the clock on the bulkhead. It showed after ten o'clock. Way after.

Oh, wow, he thought. He stretched a big stretch and let out a yawn. *Guess I've been napping.*

In the bright light of the open hatch he saw a seagull perched.

"Nosey! That you?" The rabbit sat up. "What did you find? Anything?"

"Well," said the gull, "I found where the fish boat isn't."

G.G. opened her eyes and recognized the gull standing in the hatchway: one of the seagull poop mafia bent on tormenting her. *Geez, they got to torture me here as well?*

The gull continued, "I flew from Pier 11 to

the fish docks, then out the Gate and across to Horseshoe Cove." Nosey turned his attention to G.G. "No sign of your boat, G.G."

Bunz said, "You checked around Richardson's Bay and the East Bay?"

G.G. looked toward the rabbit. *Who is this Guy?* She wondered. *And look at those ears! Longer than mine.*

Doc broke in to say, "Got food here, anyone wants it. And coffee!"

Doc picked up three mugs full of hot coffee and turned from the counter. Nosey took aim and, with a lightning strike, snagged the cherry Danish.

Doc glared. "It is *not* all for you, Nose."

With his elbow, he pushed the pastries away from the gull's perch and handed around the coffee at the banquettes.

Nosey swallowed, cleared his throat and answered Bunz's question. "Didn't get to the East Bay."

"You looking for my boat?" G.G. asked. "How do you even know it's missing?"

"Saw an empty slip near Castoffola's early this morning." Bunz blew on his coffee and watched the dog across the rim of his cup. "Nosey says you had a charter last night."

G.G. glanced at the gull. *Meddling bird,* she thought.

"With a couple of moose."

She popped Bunz a dirty look. *What made it his business?*

Bunz sipped the coffee. "And there was a dead moose floating in the bay this morning."

G.G.'s eyes bore into him. He waited. Finally she said, "Dead moose?"

"The short one," said Nosey.

G.G. shook her head, dazed. *Smilin'? Dead?* "Where?" she asked, her voice sticking in her throat.

"Pier 9," Bunz told her.

She sat back and tried to make sense of the news. She had an image of Smilin' floating, cold and lifeless in the bay. She hadn't liked the Guy, but still.

Bunz walked over to the coffee pot. His cup was still full, but he wanted to watch the dog out of her direct field of view. He poured coffee to the rim of his cup and turned. The dog's big black eyes stared back at him.

He held up the coffee pot in her direction. She shook her head. No more coffee for her.

"You don't know me. I'm Bunz." He set the pot back down. "Doc filled me in. You had quite a night."

G.G. said nothing.

"What can you tell me about these moose?"

"What do you care?" G.G. shot back.

"Don't you care? One of them seems to have your boat."

She fixed her eyes on him. *Another meddler,* she thought.

"How about their names?" Bunz waited. "Can you at least tell me that?"

Why are they all so interested in my problems? She glared at the heater. It was too hot. She reached over and flicked it off.

"The short one was Smilin' Moose. The other one, Moose M'Boy."

OK! Here's something usable! Bunz thought. He kept his voice calm. "Know anything about them? Why did they hire your boat?"

"I gave them a better rate, OK?" she snapped. "At least better than the other owners."

"Seen either one of them before?"

"Hah!" G.G.'s laugh was bitter. "Depends what you mean."

Bunz waited for her to continue.

She snarled a sigh. "Smilin', alright? I had a little fling with Smilin' before I found out what a sleazy cheeseball he was. The last I heard, he was sent up to the Moosegow."

Bunz leaned back against the counter. He watched and waited.

G.G. shook her head. "Then yesterday, there he was. Out of the blue. Should have turned my hose on them, like I almost did." She slumped back against the cushions. "Everything I own is on that boat."

Nobody had anything to say to that. It was

a bad situation. The only sound was the canal water lapping at the hull.

Bunz watched G.G. rub her forehead. Doc left the cabin. When he returned, he handed G.G. some aspirin. She thanked him and swallowed them with her coffee.

Bunz was thinking, *I'll ask around. Somebody will know these two. I can get arrest records from Den. Did they meet inside or maybe they already knew each other?*

Doc said, "Chances are your boat's OK. Nosey says nobody's seen it, so likely the Guy didn't beach it or collide with anyone. You think he might have gone out the Gate to sea?"

Nosey piped up. "He might have scuttled it!"

Doc sent Nosey an icy look and turned back to G.G. "Where do you suppose a Guy might go with a stolen boat? Would you say he had any local knowledge of the bay?"

G.G. said, "He knew Pier 13."

Nosey angled himself toward the food plate. Why let all that sweet loveliness go to waste?

Doc glared at the gull and made a move to get up. Nosey sat back down.

Doc looked back at G.G. "Did he know boats?"

"He operated the controls just fine when he

forced us into my skiff."

Bunz asked, "What about the other one—Smilin'?"

"What about him?" she snapped. Too many questions. Her head throbbed. "I knew him before I started working boats, OK?" Then she muttered, "Smilin' dead, my boat gone." She slumped lower.

"What time was the charter?" Bunz asked.

"They showed up late. Around eleven."

"Why did they want to go out at night?"

"I didn't ask. Far as I was concerned, they were cash-paying customers."

"Tough night to be out," said Bunz. He wanted to believe her—he liked her for being angry instead of looking for sympathy. Yet and still, there might be something she was holding back.

G.G. shivered again at the thought of her cold, wet night. But then she remembered, *Doc did come along and pick me up. That was a piece of luck.* Thinking about her rescue cheered her up a little.

"They were looking for something," she added. "Under the pier."

"Any idea what?"

"None." She sat forward. "I s'pose I'll put that call in to the Coast Guard."

"The phone booth is just up on shore," said Doc. "Hold on, I've got change." He stood and looked around at his guests. "Anybody want more coffee or anything? There's food here, G.G., you'll feel better if you eat something."

G.G. shook her head. "Not really hungry, thanks."

Bunz stepped out of Doc's way and sat back down. Nosey sidled a little step closer to the food. Doc eyed the gull. "What'd I say?" He slid the pastry plate to the far edge of the compact counter.

No point in staying, Nosey groused to himself. *All this food and I'm not getting any!*

G.G. watched the gull keep a sidelong eye on the pastry plate. *Maybe not such a bad Guy,* she thought. *Just looking out for himself.* It was almost funny, watching him eyeball the food. She allowed herself a little smile. *Maybe I am feeling better, if I care about a gull.*

G.G. stood up. Time to make that call, and go get some pancakes. Let Doc have his boat back to himself.

Bunz saw the smile on G.G.'s face and wondered what put it there. Was there something more she was holding back? He'd ask around, run a check into her background.

Doc handed her some quarters. There was another little smile.

Bunz frowned. Instinct told him she was telling the truth, but he wanted facts. Trust the dog? Not trust the dog? Time would tell.

13: Pier 40

Nosey couldn't stop ogling an alluring cheese Danish on the pastry plate. *Darn it! All this food nobody eating. How could they not be hungry?*

Out of the corner of his eye he saw G.G. move toward the hatch. His neck snaked out. The cheese Danish vanished from the plate. The bird hopped quickly out of Doc's reach. Out on the deck, the pastry was gobbled down in two bites.

As she passed the food plate, G.G. picked up a piece of juicy mango. She studied the plate for a moment and picked out a jelly donut for the gull. *I must be feeling better, doing something nice for that gull. Or maybe the whack on my head did knock me silly.*

She climbed through the hatch and joined Nosey on the small aft deck. The gull was finishing the Danish. She stood near him and slowly ate the ripe fruit. With the sunshine warm on her fur, she felt a little cheered up. Sipp's Creek was real pretty in the sunlight. Sparkling water, birds fooling around, grasses and trees waving in the light breeze. She had always pictured the creek to be more like a garbage dump than a beautiful little backwater like this.

Feeling the seagull's eye on her, she smiled at his bulging neck, full of the two pastries he had already eaten. His avaricious eye was on her donut. She handed it to him. He showed a moment of surprise before latching onto it and gulping it down. His neck bulged a little more.

Juke and Jake paddled together a little ways off and watched the dog and Nosey eating. They knew Doc brought pastries home from the diner—and later would be handing out treats. But that was later, and this was now. Envious, they sized up the width of Nosey's bulging neck.

From the deck, G.G. spied the old phone booth Doc had mentioned. It leaned into a shady corner of a dirt parking lot. A few old cars kept it company. She wiped off her paws and shook herself: time to call the Coast Guard.

Juke and Jake followed her progress down the ramp. She jumped to shore; at the phone booth she dropped in the coins and dialed the number. The two gulls edged in, pretending they weren't eavesdropping.

The Coast Guard took her information: her

name, stolen boat's name, what happened, where and when. The Coast Guard sounded professionally uninterested. No reports of any abandoned fish boats found. She didn't exactly mention that her skiff had been swamped, or that she knew about a certain body that had been picked up earlier along the city front.

Did she have a phone number? No? Her phone was on the stolen boat? Call this number back later, then. They gave her a case number. They suggested she call the police. "Thank you for calling the Coast Guard."

Click!

Gloomy again, she hung up the phone. *So much for the Coasties. Now what?*

A report from her stomach informed her that it was time to eat a real meal. Fruit was not enough. But she stood for a moment looking at the still water. She wasn't quite ready to move on.

Ambling down to the bank, she picked a spot and sat down to study the houseboats. *A houseboat could be a good place to live.* She envied the Guys who lived here. At least they had a place to go, and right on the water, too. Without her boat, she had nothing. She lived on her boat. All her stuff was on board and it was her livelihood.

She let the sun sink into her bones. *Time to pass the word around about my boat. If any of my friends find that Moose, they'll put a big hurt on that clown.*

Sigh! She just wanted her boat back. And not too screwed up, if possible. She watched the houseboat reflections squiggle in the water. It was soothing just sitting there, watching life on the canal.

She saw the rabbit appear and make his way down the waggling walkway. He made a point of giving a big, flashy wave to the guard gulls. She grinned as they abruptly took flight. They wheeled above the houseboats and settled on a roof one or two boats down from Doc's.

Bunz laughed as he waved. *Those two probably didn't sleep all night.* He glanced across at the dog sitting in the sun. He had a few more questions.

He walked up to G.G., giving her a small smile and a nod as he joined her on the bank. He sat quietly, waiting for her to say something. G.G. liked that. Too much blabbing wore her out.

She sniffed the air and enjoyed the damp earth smell mixed with the slightly fusty scent of canal water. "Sure is peaceful," she said.

"Yeah, it is," said Bunz. "Nice and peaceful. Get ahold of the Coasties yet?"

"Yeah. No one's called in anything."

"Tell them everything?"

None of your business, she thought. "Pretty much," she told the rabbit.

Bunz gave her a sideways glance.

"What!" She glared back. Her voice was loud. "I just want to find my boat. I don't want to get involved in a lot of blankety-blank red tape over something that wasn't my fault." She looked back toward the canal and her voice lowered. "I can't change what happened. What would I say? I don't even know all of it." Bitterly she added, "I knew that Smilin' was bad news."

"Why do you suppose they hired *your* boat? What about the other owners who hire out?"

"The way those two looked, I guess no one wanted to take them out. From what they said, I quoted them the best rate, and I charged them a lot, kind of hoping they'd go away."

They heard a gull call, and glanced up to see Nosey flying off toward the bay.

Bunz asked, "No clue of what those two were looking for? Not even a hint?"

"Smilin' kept starting in to blab, but the big one kept shutting him up. When we arrived off Pier 13, they went out on the deck to talk."

"And when they came back in?"

"Smilin' seemed very unhappy."

"And that's when Moose told you to row under Murkey's? He didn't just say 'under the pier'?"

G.G. paused. "Definitely he said Murkey's."

"But nothing about why?"

G.G. scowled. "For the one millionth time, no!"

Bunz sat, ruminating.

G.G. stood up. "I'm hungry."

"Oh yeah? There's a pretty good diner at Pier 40."

She looked at him and hesitated. He seemed OK, mostly, even though she didn't like the twenty questions routine. Why did he even care? He wasn't the one with the missing boat and clowns fouling his life.

She shrugged. "Let's go then. There's a different crowd there. I can pass the word; see if anybody's seen anything."

The rabbit followed her down the narrow bank path toward the bay. As they picked their way along, Bunz asked, "You usually hang out at Fisherman's Wharf then?"

"Yeah. My boat's berthed there. Been there for years, before it was my boat."

G.G. suddenly stopped and stared. Bunz followed her gaze. She was looking at the houseboat with the antlers on it. It had been too dark to see when she and Doc had rowed by earlier.

"That is weird," she said. "What's that all about?"

"Kinda gives you the creeps, huh."

G.G. gave a little shake. "Yeah it does!"

She turned and they continued on. G.G. sniffed at the smells in the air and enjoyed the mild sun on her fur. Ducks quacked. A fresh breeze blew by. She sighed another big sigh. Bunz glanced up at her.

"I guess you could say the seas have been a little rough lately," she said.

"How long have you owned the boat?"

"Couple of years—since my partner died."

"I'm sorry to hear that. You two used to fish?"

"Yeah."

"And you both knew those two that chartered your boat?"

"No!" she said emphatically. "And anyway, I only knew Smilin'. Met him when I first got to town." She shook her head at the memory. "Before I started fishing."

They crossed the canal at the 3rd Street Bridge and walked down King Street past the ballpark. A cluster of docked sailboats appeared on their right. Bunz pointed to the diner up ahead.

"That's where I thought we could eat. Do you know it?" he asked. "It's pretty good, not as good as Murkey's, of course."

"Yeah, I've been there a few times."

They walked into the small diner and looked around.

"Pretty quiet right now," Bunz said.

"Good. No waiting. I am ready for a big breakfast. These Guys serve it all day." She turned to the Guy at the counter. "Hi, Walter. Good to see you."

"'Morning, G.G. Long time, no see. What'll it be?"

She ordered a lot of everything, and coffee. Bunz ordered toast and coffee. At Murkey's he would have had a fresh carrot juice, but this place didn't serve it. Another reason to love Murkey's.

Walter joked with G.G. when she pulled out the wad of soggy money.

"So! You laundering money these days?"

"Not yet, Walter." And she told him why she was there.

Walter got serious and told her he would spread the word.

"You go sit down! Here's coffee. I'll bring the food when it's ready."

They picked up the coffee and walked to a table by the window. As they waited for their food, G.G. studied the boats. After eating, she would walk around the docks, talk to whoever she ran into.

Bunz watched her. "How'd you end up fishing, G.G.?"

She sat for a long moment and Bunz wondered if she had heard his question.

"How did I end up fishing?" She smiled to herself. "I met a Guy, of course. Isn't that what they say, it's who you know? I'd come out to the coast, just to look around and I liked it. Near the water, not too hot, not too cold, clean air. I worked different jobs, whatever I could get. Then I met this Guy with a fish boat—Johnny. I started working for him and learned stuff. How to fish, how to fix boat stuff, how to drive and navigate. I liked all of it, and we got along good. I got my captain's license and we started going fifty-fifty on everything."

Bunz sipped his coffee—it was not as good as Murkey's.

Walter brought the food. She dug into her pancakes and thought about Johnny the Joker, one of those Guys that everybody liked. And he had liked her.

Did she ever miss the old so-and-so!

She pushed pancake around her plate to sop up some syrup. "It was great while it lasted but then he got sick." Her voice cracked. "And he died. So now I got a boat."

"Maybe you know the Maartunis—Joe and his Pops?"

G.G. perked up. "Joe and Pops? Oh, yeah. They drove our boat when we went to spread Johnny's ashes. They are two great Guys. You know them?"

Well, thought Bunz. *That's a good sign, if*

she's friends with the Maartunis. "Yeah. Joe saw those two moose the other day, at the Old Anchor," Bunz said. "He told me they both seemed a little off, you know?"

"Yeah, I knew they were off," G.G. said defensively. "But I needed the work, OK? So I'm broke right now, OK? I can't even afford the little payoff those son-of-a-gun seagulls want so they won't poop on my boat." She frowned and looked away.

The door to the diner opened and they both turned to see who was coming in. It was just a couple of office types, in for an early lunch. Not boat Guys.

"Did anybody see you leave on your charter last night?"

"No. Ten-eleven o'clock at night? That's late around the docks. We had set the time for nine, but those two idiots showed up late." G.G. polished her plate with the last piece of pancake. "You know the rest."

She turned to her coffee. Bunz gazed out the window at the crowd of boats.

"You know what?" he asked. "Are you done? Let's get outta here and start asking around. Someone might know something!"

He jumped up and waited while G.G. took a last swallow of coffee.

Just as they reached the door, it banged open. A short reindeer burst into the diner, his Greek fishing cap set at a jaunty angle between his antlers. He stood in the door and looked at them with a big toothy smile.

"Howdy, Howdy! Good morning, good morning to you two! How are you this fine day? Such a lovely day it is, yah yah! I am going to have lunch, yes. That is why I come here! What about you?" He looked up at G.G. and his smile got even bigger. "My, my, but you are a big dog. Just look at you! You look like you just ate and that it was very, very good. Yah! I come this place every day almost. It is good. Very, very!"

Bunz and G.G. looked at each other and then back at the Guy. He was still standing in the open door, still talking.

"I don't know you. It's for sure that I don't. Would I remember such a big dog as you are? I would, yes, you I would remember. Tell me then, what brings you here to Mr. Gomez' place of business on such a tremendous lovely day? A rabbit with such ears and this big, big dog."

He smiled at them as though they were his long-time friends and turned to the counter. "Howdy, howdy, Mr. Gomez!" He waved at Walter working the griddle. "Here am I for lunch!" He turned back to Bunz and G.G.

"I will buy you a cup of Walter's good coffee. You must let me do this one thing. I have such a story to tell, I want to tell everybody. Mr. Gomez, three coffees, please! And what shall I eat for my good lunch today? I think to have one of your extra fine hamburgers and I will tell my story. Because for me today it was a very, very strange morning! Yes! Very, very! Never can you guess my morning." His smile widened. "Not for never!"

Bunz looked at G.G. and shrugged. The reindeer was obviously a regular and had the quality of a Guy who knew boats. They might as well start with him. Walter poured three coffees. The reindeer balanced the three cups between his hooves and led the way over to a table in the corner.

"Sit! Sit!" He set the coffees down and pulled out chairs for all. "Sit here with me and tell me, Big Dog. And you, Mr. Rabbit! What do they call you, hey? Me, they call me Finn, on account of that's where I come from: Finland, yah, yah. And you, Mr. Rabbit. I not see you before, neither. With such ears! What brings you here today, other than this fine, fine coffee?" He took a sip of his coffee. "Ahhh. Great coffee, Mr. Gomez. Great coffee here ever since you buy this place! Thank you for that!"

"We're looking—" G.G. started to say.

The diner door opened again and they all looked over. Finn waved heartily at the newcomer. "Howdy, howdy, Georgie! I thought to see you here! How's that outboard motor working for you now? Working good, you bet! Meet my new friends here. Me, myself, even I don't yet know their names." He laughed.

"Hello, Finn. Hold fast there. I got to order first."

The phone rang. Walter picked it up.

Finn turned back to his new friends. "So, Guys! Names! Names! How can we be good friends without I don't know your names!" He peered over at them and there was a moment of silence while he took another sip of his coffee.

Bunz jumped into the short silence and said, "I'm Bunz. This is G.G. We're—"

"Howdy, howdy, Bunz! Howdy, howdy, G.G.!" Finn waved his coffee cup toward them in greeting. "So happy to meet you! Georgia, that is who is there ordering her nice lunch. Me, I call her Georgie. And Walter, that is Walter there cooking while he is on the phone. He been cook here long time. Then he buy the place, so now I call him Mr. Gomez." Walter, still on the phone, waved a distracted paw at them as he heard his name. "Was it busy morning, Mr. Gomez?"

Walter hung up the phone and said, "So-so, Finn." He turned back to Georgia, took her order quickly and turned back to the grill.

"But you Guys," Finn said. "G.G.! Bunz! Tell me what bring you to this fine pier today. And me! So crazy a thing that happened this morning, you couldn't guess! Even if I give you all the time in the world plus one hour, you could not guess! Come over here to us, Georgie. Come right over and join! Here we have a chair, special for you." He pulled a chair over from an adjacent table. "Sit! Sit!" Finn looked pleased with himself as he waited for Georgia to walk over. "Sit here with us and listen to what happen today. I know you will not never guess!"

As Georgia put her coffee down and settled at the table, G.G. tried to get a word in. "We're here to—"

Finn kept talking. "Even you, Georgie, you will not guess!"

"So then tell us, Finn! We're all here waiting."

"So, yes. So, I will tell you. Yes. I come this morning in early, very, very. Like always I do. To miss the traffic, no? The traffic around here is a little terrible, I think. But not so bad as Rio. When I was in Rio—"

Georgia cut in. "We're not in Rio, Finn. Tell us what happened today."

"Yes, you are so right there," Finn laughed. "Rio this is not, and traffic here is not so bad as Rio." He looked around the table. "Have you Guys ever been to Rio?"

"Finn," said Georgia.

"Not yet," said G.G.

Walter came over and put plates of food in front of Finn and Georgia.

"We want to—" G.G. tried again.

Finn continued on as he orchestrated the mustard and onion on his hamburger. "So. Today. I come in early. I think to work on busted pump. I'm rebuilding pump."

Georgia leaned forward, ready to course-correct Finn's haphazard storytelling again, as needed. Finn picked up his hamburger and almost took a bite. But before he did, he put his hamburger back down and said earnestly, "I say, why spend good money on new pump, when old one you fix it up to be just like new? And is cheaper. Right, Georgie?"

Across the table, Georgia started to say something. Quickly Finn returned to his story.

"But, so. Yes. What happen today here, you ask. I got pump working good, I did. Perfect like new! And I think, you earn little break, Finn. So, I sit on bench outside workshop for few minute. And what do I see? Eh?"

G.G. and Bunz regarded the reindeer closely. Georgia took a bite of her sandwich.

Finn continued, "I see strange boat."

At this, Bunz glanced at G.G. She leaned forward, staring intently at the storyteller.

"So. I watch boat for little while. Nobody on it. Very strange, I think. It is not public dock. There is sign; it say: No Public Docking. Why strange boat tie up here when dock is not for public? I walk down to see what I see. I see local boat. So. Who put boat here? Where are they now? I see door to cabin is open. I call out."

G.G. gripped the edge of the table. Her breath stopped in her throat.

"No answer. What is going on here? No way to know. I am not mind reader! But!" Finn laughed. "I do know she wasn't there last night when I leave. So, maybe someone come back. All morning I check, no one come. So, just before lunch break, I call Coast Guard. Just for curiosity. To see what they say." He held his hamburger like a telephone. "And what they tell me?"

Georgia finished her sandwich and sat back to watch.

"It was reported stolen?" G.G. asked in a strangled voice.

Finn's eyes went wide. "Yah! Yah! How you did know that! You are a big dog and mind reader, too. Sure and it was! Stolen!" He looked around at his listeners. "They say this big, beautiful boat was reported stolen and only this morning, too! Can you believe it? Right here outside my workshop is stolen boat!" He shook his head and took a bite of his hamburger.

Finn talks on his 'hamburger phone'.

G.G. looked at Bunz. One tiny question left to ask. "Is it a fish boat named *Sea Dog*?" she asked.

Finn eyes widened and he choked on the bite of food he was swallowing. He stopped coughing and dropped his jaw open, staring at G.G.

"Is she fish boat name of *Sea Dog*? How you know that? You are big dog and smart, too!" Finn's eyes shone at her as he added, "Or you are a sea dog, too, and this your boat."

G.G. nodded yes, too stunned to say anything for a moment.

"Your stolen boat. Unbelievable!" Finn turned toward Georgia, a big smile spread across his face. "Mystery solved! Can you believe it, Georgie? Right here with us, right now! The *Sea Dog's* owners!! Unbelievable!"

"I'm the owner," said G.G. as she jumped up. "She's my boat! Stolen last night. Where is she? Is she OK?" G.G. rushed over to the door and pulled it open, a look in her eye commanding them to follow her.

Finn jumped up, hamburger in hand. "Mr. Gomez, you hear this? What a day!" He waved his hamburger aloft. "And I didn't even eat my lunch yet. Is my friend G.G.'s boat I find. Unbelievable!" He headed out the door. "Follow me, my friends. Mr. Gomez, we will report back later!"

Beyond the little coffee shop, the old shed at Pier 40 extended eight hundred feet out into the bay. Parallel to the shed was a long floating dock. Several sailboats for hire were tied alongside.

Finn stopped at a security gate, unlocked it and held it open for G.G. and the others. "This way, my friends!"

As they made their way along the wide wooden walkway, the far end came into view. And tied up at the very end was the *Sea Dog*, tugging gently against her mooring lines.

G.G. trotted toward her boat. She couldn't believe it. She had been preparing for the worst, but here was her boat—her life!—safe and sound. She bent and hauled on the stern mooring line, pulling the boat in close enough to climb aboard. She tightened up the slack in the line and jumped onto the deck. As her paws hit the deck she thought, *home!*

Bunz followed Finn as he climbed aboard. *Nice boat,* he thought.

Georgia was frowning at the other mooring line. "This line is fouled." She leaned over, straightened out the line and made it fast again.

"I saw that," said G.G. "But if that's all that happened, I don't care." She walked around the boat, examining everything.

Bunz watched the big dog and smiled. *She looks serious, but happy.*

Finn followed G.G. around as she examined her boat's every detail. No telling what that crazy moose had done while alone on her boat. They lifted hatches and peered below. Soon the talk got technical, about main engines and transmissions and generators and pumps and steering.

Sitting on the deck of the *Sea Dog*, Bunz contemplated the seawall. Built to protect the yachts tied up in the boat basin, it opened into the bay through a narrow passage. The *Sea Dog* was not narrow: she was a good-sized fish boat.

Is Moose more of a sailor than we think? Bunz wondered.

Georgia jumped back onto the float. "Hey, Guys. I got to get back to my varnishing. G.G., Bunz, pleasure to meet you. I'm over on the wooden sloop *Less Is More*. Drop by sometime. There's always a get-together on Friday afternoons, so don't be shy."

G.G. and Finn looked up from discussing the *Sea Dog's* bilge pump and waved.

Bunz watched her walk up the float toward shore. *Just what the Moose was doing,* he realized, *only a few hours ago. Then where did he go?*

14: Bill the Bum

Bill the Bum, semiretired moose of the shady trades, had one basic rule: vigilance at all times. In his world, it was never possible to be too vigilant. Whenever he was out, day or night, he kept his eyes peeled, his antlers on alert. Although nothing was exactly wrong with daytime, nighttime was his usual time to go out. If he had to, he would venture out when the sun was up. But he didn't make it a habit.

But today he was out, and it was a beautiful morning for a walk to the diner. His bum leg didn't ache much, and he scarcely limped.

Nice ta have an excuse ta get out, get some air, he thought. His eyes swept the terrain; his antlers probed the empty-headed breeze for shreds of trouble. But all seemed quiet.

The diner at Pier 40 was the only place left that he liked to frequent. It had been around longer than him. Just for that, he loved the joint. Maybe he stayed in too much. But where else would he go, all by himself?

When he had a little extra cash, he would

splurge at the diner. He got tired of his own cooking, just like his guests probably did. But he hated spending his own money when he didn't have to. Sometimes, on a good day like today, one of his occasional guests would pay. And today, Moose M'Boy wanted a big ol' breakfast, and Moose was paying. So here he was, out in the morning, hungry and looking forward to a good breakfast.

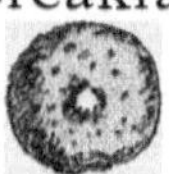

Bunz relaxed in the sun and watched the water lap at the seawall. What was the chain of events last night, he mused. How did Moose pilot the stolen boat to this narrow gap into the harbor—in that fog—steer safely through the gap, maneuver to the dock and tie up? By himself? It only made some sense if he'd done it before.

According to Doc, Moose had shown up at the diner around 4 a.m. It was a thirty to forty-minute walk to Murkey's from here. Bunz looked back at shore. So where did he go, say, between one a.m. and four this morning?

"Hey, G.G.!" Bunz leapt up. "Quick! Check this out!"

G.G. poked her head up from below deck. "Is that your Moose M'Boy?"

"Wait a sec." She climbed up on deck and looked to where the rabbit pointed. "Hold on.

I'll get the binoculars." From the wheelhouse, she peered toward shore. "Nope. Not him. But it sure is a moose."

A third moose, Bunz thought.

"Finn?" She handed the binoculars to Finn. "Do you know this Guy?"

Finn waved off the binoculars. "Yah, yah, that Guy, him I know. Bill the Bum, he is. He have some history. You know that Sipp's Creek? He live there, with those other bums and rowdies." Finn lowered his voice. "Walter tell me he have antlers nailed to houseboat! Antlers of dead moose." He shuddered and shook his own antlers.

"So, he's the one," said Bunz softly. He tried to catch G.G.'s eye, but she was busy sorting through her toolbox. She had no interest in moose unless it was M'Boy.

Finn added, "Me, I don't go near to that creek. Not never! Walter, he tell me antlers are from dead friends of that Bill." Toward Bill he called out, "Me, I am not moose! And I am not your friend! I am reindeer!"

Though Bill was too far away to hear, he glanced in their direction. Finn quickly turned away. "You find wrench?" he asked G.G.

So ho! Bunz thought. *A third moose, and he lives just a short walk away. That could be why M'Boy left the fish boat here.*

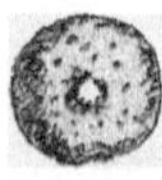

Walter looked up as Bill pushed open the door.

"Mornin', Walter!"

"Morning, Bill. How's the tail shakin'? Kinda early for you, ain't it?" Walter flipped a grilled cheese and did not see Bill scowl at this remark on Bill's habits. "What'll it be today?"

"I'll have my usual. And gimme a full stack a' blueberry pancakes, three eggs scrambled and home fries. And toss in a couple a' them grilled cheese and two tuna. Ta go."

"Gotcha, Bill. Somebody's hungry, huh?"

"Yeah. Someone's always hungry somewhere, ain't they? An' I'll take a cuppa yer coffee while I'm waitin'."

Bill took his coffee over to a table with a good view of the surroundings. With his back to the wall, he waited for his food. The place wasn't half full, but he couldn't relax. He kept an eye on the door and thought about his own boring cooking. Maybe he should take one of them cooking classes for bachelors.

G.G. found the wrench she wanted and she and Finn went back to their discussion below deck.

"Hey, Guys!" B. called down to them. The talking stopped.

"Yeah, Bunz," G.G. answered.

"You all right here? I'm taking off."

"OK." G.G. stuck her head out of the hatch and looked at Bunz for a long moment. "Bunz. Thanks isn't enough, but thanks for your help. You have no idea."

She shook her head. Maybe a little tear glistened in her eye.

"G.G., you gotta thank Finn here, really. And Doc. Plus, don't forget. You helped me, too."

As Bunz leaped to the walkway, his ears flew out behind him. The walkway wobbled when he landed and he paused for it to settle. He called back to the boat, "Stop by later at Murkey's, you Guys. Late afternoon, OK?" He heard a muffled acceptance as he set off down the float.

Bunz felt fired up. This gimpy old moose might just lead him to the treacherous Moose M'Boy.

Through the diner window, Bill watched a rabbit amble slowly down the walkway toward the diner—a rabbit who pretended to study the sailboats. Bill's antlers tingled.

He stood up and strolled over to the grill to see how the food was coming along. Still the same ol' monster grill from when he first came in the place. During the forty years he had lived around the waterfront, a lot had changed, but not that grill. Putting up that darn ballpark had ruined the whole area. When he thought back, it was hard to believe how much had been torn down or turned into condos for snotty rich punks.

Thought the world was their oyster, with no clue how hard a regular Guy had ta work just to get by. They'd find out. Life wasn't all fat paychecks and overpriced gadgets.

Bill had his little schemes for getting by, but keeping it all under the radar, that was taking more effort these days. He thought back to the Sugar Ban. That had been plush times, it had. Them two-bit politicians had finally done something right, by golly. Everyone on the take, and a Guy who knew the score could really make out good. Bill had learned a few lessons by then and had stashed a lot of that easy cash away, 'stead of spending it as soon as he got it. He chuckled to himself. Good times, indeed!

The food ready, Bill left a small tip and picked up the bags. As he eased the door closed, he casually glanced around. He didn't make a big deal of looking around, but look carefully he did. He didn't see the rabbit. Not right off. Not seeing him made Bill more suspicious as he turned south along the yacht basin, toward the canal.

Where was that rabbit?

15: Results at the Library

Special to the Post

Dex Dexter

Late last night a minor fender bender turned into a big collar for the cops. Allegedly, faulty truck brakes gave Sugar Patrol Investigators a new angle on sugar smuggling, long known to trouble our waterfront. And Murkey's, that popular local dive on Pier 13, port of call for local longshoremen and sailors the world over, played a part.

We are told that the delivery truck involved in the late-night accident, owned by city trucking and contracting business Duck Contractors, was unable to avoid a street light pole in front of Murkey's. When the driver, also a part-time employee at Murkey's, went inside the eatery to use the phone, the truck's rear loading door was jimmied and contents from the back of the truck were stolen. From a burst-open bag left inside the truck, Investigators responding to the accident discovered that bags labeled as 'Cement' were actually filled with pure cane sugar. The driver was detained for questioning.

Twenty minutes after this incident was reported, in what at first appeared to be an ordinary traffic stop further north along the docks, city police detained a car after it ran a stop sign near Pier 33. The driver of the car turned out to be one Moose M'Boy, a character already known to the authorities. A search of his vehicle produced two large bags labeled 'Cement.' Through radio contact, the officers determined that the sacks matched those discovered in the crashed truck at the diner. Mr. M'Boy was arrested at the scene.

Contacted by the Post, George 'Big' Duck, the owner of Duck Contractors, was unaware of the theft of one of his trucks or its part in these illegal activities last night. Mr. Duck says he deplores the use of his trucks for anything illegal. He plans to immediately increase security personnel at his truck lot, long located south of Market Street. According to our Sugar Unit contact, this is not the first incident of stolen trucks being commandeered to transport contraband.

Webbs looked up from squinting into the microfiche reader and grinned. Success! After crawling through old precinct newsletters and jotting down possible incidents that happened near Murkey's, he used the dates to comb through old newspapers in the microfiche.

And now he'd found a real clue in black and white: a moose, a robbery and a crashed truck, during the last days of the Sugar Ban— all right in front of Murkey's! What a slick scam: Pack the sugar in cement bags, move it around in business trucks. If someone gets caught, the owner claims the truck was stolen. Foolproof. Only here was a fool who got caught, in fact, TWO fools were caught—but no one to track the stuff back to, as long as the fools kept their traps shut. Pretty neat. What if there was more to this newspaper story than just a little sugar smuggling?

Webbs thought back. The accident seemed minor at the time. It hadn't crossed his mind since. That night he had been at Rufus Cain's, helping him with his little stealth baking business. Good old Rufus, who had saved enough to open his own bakery just before the Sugar Ban messed it up. No one had ever thought the Sugar Ban would become law.

The spider felt a presence by his shoulder. When he looked up, he saw Marilyn, the librarian, smiling and holding two books. The little bow on her head danced; her glasses slid down her nose.

"Webbs! Look at these books! *Prohibition on the West Coast,* published in 1938. I found it misfiled, next to this book about the old shanghai days, which has a whole chapter on tunnels! And both have at least some descriptions of tunnels under the city, that lead to the waterfront!"

Webbs' smile broadened. "Tunnels? Really?" He reached for the Prohibition book. "Fantastic!"

Suddenly a memory popped into Webbs' brain. Gran'dad had made up stories for him, about the adventures of Eek and Ike, two mice who lived in the tunnels under the city. Eek and Ike smuggled cheese into the tunnels to eat during the cold winters. Maybe Gran'dad wasn't making it all up!

Marilyn waved *Shanghai Days* under his nose. "Check this out, Webbs! This book claims some of the shanghai tunnels were later fixed up and used to smuggle booze."

"No kidding! You hit the jackpot, kiddo!"

"Think about it—small boats smuggled most of the alcohol into the bay. Some fishermen used their fish boats to make extra money! They knew the local waterways better than anyone. A bootleg boat drops off product at a tunnel that connects to the bay. It leads under the city to the cellar doors of different speakeasies. With speakeasies all over town, it's the perfect back door delivery system!"

"How much you want to bet the tunnels were used for sugar 'legging, too?" said Webbs.

He tapped the microfiche machine. "You should read this, Marilyn! There's a moose caught with sugar on the wharf. If it's one of our moose, then maybe we are on to something! Read it and tell me what you think."

Webbs flipped through the Prohibition book while Marilyn read the article. "I'd guess that Guy caught with the sugar sacks was sent to prison, and maybe the truck driver, too," she said.

"If that truck driver is the Guy I'm thinking of, he worked as a dishwasher for a couple months. A skinny moose."

"Did Murkey's ever use real sugar? Could he have been bringing sugar to the diner?"

"Well, smuggling kinda went unmentioned at the diner, if you know what I mean. If they knew you, you could get real pastry, because really, who wants a donut made with fake sweetener? Did you ever try that stuff?" He shuddered. "Terrible!"

Marilyn read off the date of the article. "If these two were both sent to prison, of course we don't know for how long. But just say something kept them away till now. The question becomes, why come back?"

"Yup. That's the question." Webbs flipped pages, hoping to find maps. "Let's say there is a tunnel near Murkey's, and it was used for smuggling. That could mean rumors about Sprinkhels Junior smuggling his own sugar are true. Which might explain why Junior doesn't sell the place."

"You mean there might be evidence of past crimes? No one really cares about those old crimes anymore, unless you're nuts like us." She giggled. "Those smuggling rumors make the Sprinkhels family seem kind of glamorous to me."

Webbs looked up. "What's so funny?"

"I was thinking. Someone could start a walking tour of the tunnels. Charge admission!"

They both laughed.

"Yeah! A Segway tour," the spider said sarcastically. "The Shanghai Days Pub and Tunnel Crawl. But seriously, do you suppose the tunnels are part of the puzzle? That the moose is here because—I don't know, maybe something in his past?"

"Here's another possibility," said Marilyn. "Not the tunnel itself, but something in the tunnel."

Webbs picked up the idea. "Yeah! That the moose knows about and the Sprinkhels family is trying to hide, and that's why they hold onto the diner. And the moose wants it, or is threatening blackmail or something."

"We need to find out about this other character, the truck driver. Do you remember that dishwasher's name?"

"No. But Hamms would." Webbs closed his book and put it down. "It's disappointing that these books don't have maps. We need maps. We need information on these characters and a list of Sprinkhels' downtown properties. We match up the properties with the map of the tunnels and see if they align."

Webbs reached for his pencil and started a list:

- Tunnel map

- Sprinkhels building locations

- Did Sprinkhels know Duck Contractor owner?

- Is Moose M'Boy or other moose in the article either of the moose Ida saw?

- Who was truck driver, did he work at Murkey's—ask Hamms

- Other news reports

- Does Bunz remember the truck accident?

Webbs could feel Marilyn staring at him.

"Guess what time it is, Webbs." She was smiling a big smile.

"Huh?" He looked around. "Time?"

"I have an idea. And anyway," she tapped her watch, "it's quitting time!" She looked at him confidently. "Why can't we find out if there's a tunnel near Murkey's? You and me! Now. Didn't you notice how this all centers around the diner? It's time for spiders underground!"

Webbs looked dubious, so she added, "And after, you can introduce me to Murkey's!"

Put like that, Webbs thought, it was a great idea!

16: Two Moose

As Bill the Bum ambled past the yacht basin, Bunz trailed behind. *Looks like that moose is carrying enough food for two Guys his size.* Keeping the gimpy moose barely in view, the rabbit hung way back. But pretty soon he could feel it—somehow the moose had spotted him.

Shoot. I'm off my game! Now what? He made some quick calculations. *I'll turn down Berry Street and go around the inland side of ballpark. He's slow—I can make the canal ahead of him. He either crosses one of the bridges or stays on the north side and passes right by me. If Finn is right, that's Bill's houseboat with the antlers. He may have a separate, secret hidey-hole for dodgy guests like M'Boy. Only one way to find out!*

Without another glance at Bill, the rabbit turned inland. As soon as the moose was out of his sight, he put on some speed.

In a far corner of his eye, Bill saw the rabbit turn off. *That's a rabbit on a mission,* he groused to himself. He shook his antlers and swished his stubby tail.

Took just one rabbit ta ruin a perfec'ly good mornin'. Bill kept on, pretending all was normal. He passed the ballpark, and headed to where the canal emptied into the bay. He turned right and followed along the canal bank to the 3rd Street Bridge.

An' that moron Moose M'Boy. Whatever he thinks he's doing, he's obviously mucked it up. Must have, if he needs a place ta lay low, and him jus' outta the Moosegow. Fresh outta stir, and he's moosin' around the same waterfront where they pinched him. An' what result? Trouble fer me. But honestly, Bill, old sod, did ya ever trust that one? And what about Smilin' Moose—another dim bulb. If he's not with M'Boy, where then?

Juke and Jake had told Bill yesterday that they had seen those two pallin' around all week. The extra sandwiches were for the gulls. Bill hoped they had more info for him when he got back.

In the middle of the 3rd Street Bridge, Bill paused. He looked up the canal toward the houseboats and the 4th Street Bridge. No rabbit. His eyes swept the scene as he turned to look toward the bay. No rabbit in sight.

So, I maybe was wrong about that rabbit and maybe not. Still feelin' jumpy. Just have ta keep extra sharp.

Bill crossed over the bridge and headed inland on the canal path, the same little path Bunz and G.G. had taken earlier. Without swiveling his head around, he paid careful attention to every little movement, out to the edges of his vision. He neither saw nor smelled anything like a rabbit nearby, but his antlers were tingling. He frowned at the thought of Moose waiting inside for his breakfast.

Guests are welcome only so long as they don't bring no trouble. There I draw the line. And it ain't no stinkin' line in no sand.

When he reached the floating walkway, he looked around for Juke and Jake. He spied them inland past the houseboats, down where the canal dead-ended under the freeway.

Well, too far away right now. I'll snag 'em later.

Bill the Bum dumped the food bags onto his scarred kitchen counter and flicked off the dim ceiling light. Binoculars hung on a nail next to an old window curtain streaked with grease. The binoculars had been new some time ago and showed their age, but they were of best quality, a memento from one of the first jobs he had pulled. As he reached for them, his anger flared. His tail flicked slowly back and forth.

I shouldn't have ta worry like this! I'm semi-retired fer Pete's sake.

Using the binoculars to hold the curtain aside, he scanned the opposite side of the canal for rabbits. Empty. He did one more slow pass through the little window.

Behind him, Moose eased into the dark kitchen. His eyes cut over toward Bill leaning across the counter, peering out the window. He saw Bill's tail shift back and forth. The back of Moose's neck prickled.

"Morning, Bill," Moose said. "How's the world out there?"

Bill said nothing, just flicked his tail.

"Food smells good!" Moose moved in closer to Bill. "What we got here?" He tilted a food bag toward the paltry window light and looked in. Bill snapped the binoculars onto the counter. The curtain swung shut.

Here's trouble, Moose thought. He took a slow breath, picked up the bags, and turned toward the table. Casually he said, "Something I should know, Bill?" Moose put the food bags on the table and pulled plastic utensils and napkins from the bags. He sniffed at the sandwiches.

Bill flicked on the dim light and leaned against the sink, hard eyes on his guest.

"Tell me," Bill said harshly. "Does that look like pancakes? Them sandwiches is fer the gulls."

"So, OK, Bill." Moose set the sandwiches

on the table and, holding his temper, he faced Bill. "Keepin' up ta date with them gulls, are ya?"

"With you around, looks like I have ta."

The two stared at each other. Moose spoke first.

"Keep yer antlers on, Bill. What's got yer dander smokin'?"

"*You* wanna know what's got *my* dander smokin'? That's rich, that is!" His tail switched faster. "What's goin' on, Moose! Yer in town a few days, an' already ya gotta hide out. Why? I go out fer food—fer you!—and I pick up a tail. Why?"

Bill glared at his guest. Moose snarled, "A tail? Ya brought a tail back here?"

"A rabbit followed me. With real long ears."

"Don't know any rabbits, Bill."

"Maybe not, but a rabbit knows you. Gotta be you."

Moose snatched up the binoculars, pushed past Bill and thrust the window curtain aside. Behind him, Bill angrily flicked off the light.

Moose studied the canal and the bank on the other side. "I don't see nothin', Bill."

The curtains swung back into place. Moose flipped the light on.

"Not now. He took off. Knew I spotted 'im. But get this!" Bill smacked a hoof on the countertop. "I ain't lookin' fer no trouble on account a' yer ignorant arse!"

Moose's rancor simmered. *Not this! Not now! Just when I figger how ta get at my stash.* His stomach growled. He needed something to eat and a minute to think.

"How 'bout I put some water on fer coffee an' we talk?" Moose walked over to the stove and lifted the heavy iron kettle. He headed toward the sink.

Bill slid into his way and snarled, "What ya gone an' done, Boyo?"

Moose shook his big head and stopped. "Ain't done nothing, Bill." He bumped the heavy kettle against his leg. His stomach growled again. "I'm makin' coffee."

"Screw coffee." Bill snorted and stamped a hoof on the deck, louder than he meant to. "Ya ain't got time fer coffee, Boyo."

"Hah!"

"Yer done here."

Moose hefted the kettle and took a step forward. "I stay till dark."

"I say yer done, then y'are done!"

"Think again!" Moose made as if he were ignoring Bill and walked around him. He set the kettle in the sink and turned on the water, holding himself poised for an attack from his bristling host. He watched the kettle fill. He'd already decided: *I hit Murkey's after dark, then high tail it straight outta town. Bill or no*

Bill, I'm spendin' the day here.

Moose eased past the glowering Bill and set the heavy kettle on the stove. He flicked the flame on. "Where ya keep yer coffee, Bill?"

Bill snatched up a canister of coffee. "Coffee? Ya want coffee?" He flung it straight at Moose. "Here!"

Moose did a quick sidestep. The canister banged onto the deck and slid behind him. Moose lifted the heavy kettle from the flame and squared around to face Bill.

"Cool it, Bill."

Bill's tail flashed back and forth. "Cool it, nuthin'! Take yer food an' go! And don't come back!"

Moose tightened his grip on the kettle. "I stay till after dark."

"Fergit whose place this is? Ya lost privilege, which means out ya go! Now!"

"Till dark, Bill." He stared at Bill. "There's a good reason."

"Screw reasons, Boyo. Yer done and double done!"

Moose expanded to his tallest. "Ya think I'm gonna go out there jes' ta pull a rubberneck rabbit off yer place?" He stared into Bill's eyes. A grain of an idea came to him.

Bill sneered and opened his mouth, but Moose spoke first. "I come back fer sumthin'. It's big."

Bill's eyes followed Moose as he set the kettle back on the flame.

"Important big. And I need a Guy, a partner."

"I heard ya had one," Bill said snidely.

"That Guy," Moose said dismissively, "He's out. I need a Guy I can count on."

Bill said, "No kiddin'." His angry stance eased back a tiny bit. What did Moose have going on?

Moose pushed his advantage. "Ya don't want in, I leave ta-morrow. Ya want in? We talk."

The kettle began to steam.

Bill eyed Moose. "About what?"

Got 'im! thought Moose. "Jes' hold on there a minute, Bill. Lemme have a look-see out the front, see if that rabbit's out there. Then we talk."

Moose reached for the binoculars. He could feel the greed working in his host. Bill snatched up the binoculars first and said, "Make yer damn coffee." He headed down the hall.

Smug with victory, Moose called after him, "Best damn coffee yez ever had, Bill!"

From the hallway he heard Bill call softly, "Quit yelling."

An hour later, Moose tipped his chair back, satisfied. He loved a good breakfast. He looked across the littered table at Bill. No food was left. Bill would have ta get something else fer the gulls.

"So, that's what's going on, Bill. More coffee?" He reached back and lifted the coffee off the stove.

"Yeah, a'right. Ya do make good coffee, fer a fact." Bill pushed his cup across to Moose.

Moose filled Bill's cup. As he laid out his plan for Bill, he could see how good it was. *Get a car—ya had a clear line of sight inta the diner from the curb. Middle a the night, no one there; we slip in. Bill holds down the kitchen help, I buzz underneath, grab the stash, off we drive. Fifteen-twenty minutes tops. Maybe less.*

Moose picked his teeth and watched Bill.

"We still got that rabbit ta worry about," Bill said

Moose got up to examine the other side of the canal again. "Don't see 'im."

"Don't mean he ain't out there though," Bill said. He looked at Moose speculatively. "Do I have this straight? Ya stashed a haul under Murkey's and then got popped right after that, fer sugar smugglin'?

"That's about it."

"An' ya been inside fer ten years?"

"Yep. An' believe me, that's a long time when ya break it down inta hours."

Bill shook his head. *What a dumbo.* "And

why would yer stash still be there?"

Moose smiled. "Don't worry. I tucked it in nice an' snug. I jes' need ta get at it."

"An' if I help ya, what would the split be?"

Moose held his toothpick out for inspection and saw that both ends were shot. He could still feel something stuck between his back teeth. "Ya got any floss?"

"Yeah, I got floss. What about the split?"

"What about the floss?"

Bill stalked out and returned with a roll of floss. He watched Moose work the floss between his big back teeth. Moose's plan was stupid. Plain stupid. He had a way better idea.

Moose held up the floss to see what had been stuck. Blueberry skin from the pancakes.

"Well?" said Bill.

"I figger the whole job takes twenty minutes tops. Plus the count-out after. That's worth, say, much as twenty per cent, Bill."

Bill laughed loudly.

"What!?" asked Moose.

"Number one, yer idea? It's stupid. Did ya ever hear a' cops and donuts? How do we know a cop don't walk in? Number two, yer stupid if ya think I'm gonna do anything fer twenty percent."

Moose's temper flared. *Now that Bill knew there was a stash, he was gonna take advantage.*

Bill could see Moose get heated. He didn't care. "An' number three, I have a better idea." He sneered. "Ya say the stash ain't even inside the diner. Why go in at all?"

Moose scowled. "So what's yer great idea?"

Bill beamed back a snarky grin. "I got a easy way ta get beneath the diner."

"Yeah?"

"Yeah. No cliff climbin' down that Embarcadero wall, no boats, no diner."

Moose tipped his chair back. What was Bill getting at?

"Jus' look at yerself, Moose. Right now, ya got nothin'. My plan's good, but I ain't givin' it away fer no twenty percent. Here ya are, at my place fer free. Gettin' my know-how is not free. It's worth fifty percent."

Moose's chair hit the deck with a thunk. *Unbelievable! The sleazy, rat-faced son of a coat factory wasn't just taking advantage. He was taking over!*

Bill repeated, "At least fifty percent."

"Fifty percent?" choked Moose. *He tried to think—how many ways could there be to get under that diner? What had he missed?*

"Maybe I could see thirty-seventy."

"Hah! Fer thirty-seventy ya can go stay somewheres else. An' find another fool ta get tailed fer ya!" Bill shoved his chair back from the table. *What a clown!*

Moose looked at Bill a long time. *The ways a Guy could skin ya, just 'cause he had an edge! Bill's sittin' there so sure a hisself. Maybe I'll jes' snuff 'im now and move on. But what if he does have a better scheme?*

Moose sighed. "What da ya say ta forty-sixty?"

With one big motion, Bill swept all the table trash into a beat-up metal can.

"Yer a joker, Moose. Go pack yer stuff. Oh, wait!" Bill glowered at Moose. "Ya ain't got nothin' ta pack." He reached for the binoculars and started cleaning them with a paper napkin. He felt completely unconcerned. It could go either way. He would have a place to stay. Moose would not.

Moose steamed. *I got my guns. On the other hand, Bill would be a tolerable partner till the job was done. He pro'lly had a good plan at that. He was an old pro and he knew the city real good.*

Bill examined his cleaning results in the weak light. "I get fifty percent or no go."

Moose gave out with a hollow laugh. "Ha-ha. OK, Bill. Ya drive a hard bargain. If yer idea's any good, we go fifty-fifty." *And ya git ta hold yer fifty percent fer a whole minute 'fore I plug yer bloody lights.*

Moose pushed himself up straight. "So. Tell me what ya got in mind, Bill."

17: Tunnels

"Tunnels?" said Moose. He struggled to keep his voice from quavering. "Underground tunnels?"

Bill gave a short, harsh laugh. "That's where they usually put 'em, Boyo. Scared a' the dark?" he sneered.

Not the dark. Moose liked the dark. But why should he allow Bill to isolate him in an unknown warren and lead him who-knows-where through tangled tunnels? Could he rely on this same Bill to lead him back out, after they recovered the stash? No, sir!

Moose steeled himself: "How long in the tunnel, Bill?"

"Ohhh," Bill grinned in his face, "can't rightly say. They ain't straight." He leaned back and relished Moose's dilemma. "Might take a hour."

Moose ignored his hectoring host. *OK, Moose. Think about it. Ya pro'lly got but one more shot fer yer cash. Ya already struck out twice. This could really work. It don't involve but one other Guy. An' this way ya can't be seen from the street. Ya string along th' old grinder, then leave him in the tunnels fer th' rats.*

Moose moved to get up from the kitchen table. "Let's get goin', then."

"Cool yer jets, hotshot." Bill reached behind himself and picked up a small pamphlet from the counter. "We wait 'til low tide. Le' see." He scanned columns of tiny numbers in the tide table. "Coupla hours."

"Low tide?" Moose's jaw dropped.

"Ha-haa!" Bill laughed at Moose and the expression on his face. "Re-lax! Back when they filled in Mission Bay here, they went cheap on the fill. After the last big earthquake, the fill sank down here an' there. The tunnel entrance at this end, when the tide's in, it gets a little water in it, is all." His eyes taunted Moose. "Just yer hooves'll get wet, Boyo."

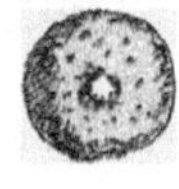

Webbs and Marilyn stood on the top of the seawall next to Murkey's and looked down at the choppy water. The afternoon breeze blew along The Embarcadero at a good fifteen knots. Webbs held one leg on his hat to keep it from flying off. The sun, heading west behind them, cast shadows of the city across the pavement behind them.

Webbs grinned over at Marilyn. An excited

smile spread across her face. About seven feet below them, the end of a large culvert stuck its rusty butt end out through the concrete retaining wall separating the city from the bay.

"Look at that! What did I tell you, Webbs?"

"Maybe yes, maybe no, Marilyn. Could be it's just an old drainage pipe."

As they crawled down the wall, the breeze ruffled their spider fur. They reached the top of the culvert and looked around. Webbs noticed the wet band left by the ebbing afternoon tide. Above it was the high-water mark, deposited from all the years of tides coming in and out of the bay.

To their right were columns of pier pilings holding up Pier 13, their upper portions weatherworn to a silvery patina. Lower down, where the tidal waters came and went, they were covered with a green slime that glowed bright in the afternoon light.

Marilyn poked Webbs. "Hey! Take a look at that thing!" She pointed beneath the pier.

"Wow! The old stair!" Webbs said.

The skeleton of an iron stairway hung down, its upper end connected to the pier structure by a giant spring hinge. This mechanism, which had once moved the stair up and down to the water, was now sculpted by rust and beyond repair. The wood steps had splintered to nothing. The disintegrating handrail hung useless in the air. Water dripped slowly as the low tide surged beneath.

"That's what Gran'dad called the 'Smuggler's Friend.' See, they used to swing it down to the water with that spring when the smuggling boats came by. And there, at the top, where it attaches, that's the hatch into the kitchen at Murkey's. They brought the stuff up directly into the diner kitchen."

He looked at Marilyn. His excitement showed in her eyes. "The stories Gran'dad told me, I thought they happened long ago. Now I'm wondering. Might be he did a little smuggling himself back in the day!" He looked again at the ruined stair.

"From here, they could easily truck the stuff all over town," she said.

The scent of pastries tickled Webbs' nose. He gazed up longingly at the diner. "When we're done, we're getting donuts, right?"

Marilyn smiled and nodded. She smelled it, too. "So, let's see about this culvert."

With a fancy little spider move, they swung into the culvert and peered into the void.

"Wow!"

Gloom smudged everything, but deep inside, they saw a rough metal wall fitted to the curve of the culvert, blocking off passage into the interior. A door had been set in the center.

"Did you bring a flashlight?" Webbs asked.

"Yup. Right here. New batteries!"

"Got mine, too. Batteries aren't new, but they'll do."

They clicked on the flashlights and ran the light beams across the door. It was a heavy old steel hatch that had once been part of an old ship. A massive padlock, as big as the spiders, fastened it closed. At the bottom edge of the door, the culvert curved down, leaving a narrow gap. Through this gap, water trickled out and splashed into the bay. Rust covered everything.

They looked at each other. This was no ordinary storm drain.

"Oh, wow!" Marilyn sighed happily. "Already better than I'd hoped."

"You said it! That lock looks solid, but I think we can get in through that gap at the bottom."

"Yeah. I know I can. But you're bigger than I am, Webbs," Marilyn teased her friend. "But maybe all that fur will flatten down and you can make it, too."

They crawled to the door and stood beside the water trickle. A flow of air from the tunnel side escaped through the gap. They poked their flashlight beams through the gap and peered into darkness. Their lights sparkled on the water. Beyond that, nothing was detectable.

They turned to each other, excited, and a little apprehensive. Who knew what might be on the other side?

"Well, here goes." Webbs set his hat down and through the gap he pushed his flashlight ahead of him.

Hoof deep in Sipp's Creek, Moose waivered. To just look into the drainage pipe, he had to stoop. Though he was still standing in the bright sun, the cramped darkness gave him the pea-green collywobbles. He shuddered.

Ahead of him, thirty feet in, Bill looked back.

"Ain't cha coming, Champ? Awwww, don't tell me yer scared." He shook his antlers and adjusted his tool pouch decisively. "Come on, Big Boy" he growled. "Let's do this! Tide won't wait." Bill limped onward, his flashlight beam gleaming off the slime.

Moose grimaced and ducked his head. But not enough. Thwak! His antlers cracked into the low vault of the culvert. A nerve in his neck pinged. He clenched his teeth and bent lower. His stomach did a grim flip as he took a last breath of fresh air.

Bill was going to pay for this. Big Time!

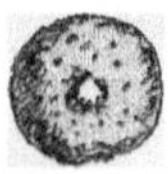

Webbs crouched next to the water trickle. Avoiding the water as much as possible, he squeezed through the gap under the door. From the other side, Marilyn passed his hat through. He adjusted it back on his head and picked up his flashlight. Marilyn slid easily underneath. Behind them, little gleams of light slipped through the rust holes in the makeshift wall, reflecting off the water.

They were so nervous and excited, the flashlight beams shook as they shone them around. Twenty feet down the tunnel, the rotted frame of a chair collapsed against the sidewall. Beyond it, the culvert angled up and headed westerly, perhaps going straight through the entire city, all the way to Ocean Beach. Who knew?

"This is an entire underground realm," said Webbs.

"Doesn't look that fancy to me. More like an isolated ambit," said Marilyn.

"OK, Ms. Librarian." Webbs took a breath of tunnel air. "Not too stinky, is it? Smells like adventure!" he joked.

"It is a little creepy, though" said Marilyn. "But no one's going to bother a couple of spiders, right?"

"Well, who's gonna be down here?" Webbs pointed out. "I mean, these days? There probably hasn't been anybody in these old tunnels for years and years."

"And what's an adventure without a little spice, right?" Marilyn said as she aimed her light at the chair. "What do you guess? Someone used to sit watch here when they were moving sugar?"

"Possible. It's been here a while—look how rotted out it is." Webbs played his light around. "Where do you suppose a secret vault would be built in?"

"Well, probably not here," she said, looking at the slick walls. "Too wet."

"True. Look at the water line. Gets kinda deep in here at high tide."

Marilyn started down the tunnel. "Let's get going, see where this thing takes us."

Off they went, edging alongside the water trickle.

"You know, if there was more water, we could race a couple of these sticks down it," said Marilyn.

"Too much trash," Webbs replied. "On the other hand, there will be plenty of water when the tide comes in." He shuddered. "Let's keep moving. We need to be out of here before then."

18: The Light of Day

As soon as Bunz saw Bill the Bum vanish into his houseboat, he withdrew. Next stop, Murkey's. The rabbit was in an agreeable mood as he strolled along The Embarcadero. Maybe it was the sunny afternoon and the faintly salty, funky smell of the bay. Mostly it was because he'd made some progress on the moose trail. There was one other thing: G.G. The dog had been so thrilled when she found her boat. She obviously loved that boat, loved it too much to risk it on dodgy deals. It appeared that she had told a straight story and really was a good dog. Those two names she'd given him were gold. Now a third name was added to the picture: Bill the Bum. What were these moose up to?

He planned to give Den a call at the precinct and ask him to look up the records of Moose M'Boy, Bill the Bum and Smilin' Moose. The records would tell him something, but not what drew the moose to Murkey's last night. M'Boy had made two moves on the diner in just a few hours. No reason he wouldn't try again, and soon.

For now, he'd gotten away clean, but M'Boy had to be feeling pressured. Did he figure G.G. and Smilin' were dead? Maybe he ditched those two in the fog because he believed they had gone ashore and talked. Or maybe he thought they were dead and that was why he took off with the fish boat. Added to that were the Guys who'd seen him in the diner. How far did this moosed-up maneuver go? No way to know.

Those wiseacres weren't going to beat him to the punch again.

Up ahead, Murkey's sign hove into view. Instead of going inside, Bunz passed the diner and angled over to the seawall that ran between the piers. He hopped to the top of the wall and looked over. There was a stretch of very smooth concrete all the way down to the ebbing tide. No way could a moose get down there from up here.

Of course, neither can I. Not without a ladder!

Bunz studied the culvert sticking out from the wall. He looked at the pier, now several feet above the tide. *G.G. said that M'Boy sent them under the pier last night, to Murkey's. Could they have been heading for that stair? Suppose M'Boy knows about that stair.*

Then it hit him! Sure! The moose had been a sugar 'legger, one of the grunts who loaded sugar, stood lookout, took a spell at the wheel when the captain needed a break. That's how he knew the yacht club! That would put him in and out of the yacht club a hundred times, in the dark, in the fog. Maybe M'Boy didn't think like a sailor, but plainly he knew boats.

Bunz knew the yacht club, too. It had been on his old sugar beat. His Pie Inspector Team always suspected it was a regular smugglers' drop. Suspected, hell! They knew it was. But wealthy citizens who owned creamy yachts and downtown real estate had a lot of drag at City Hall. Drag at City Hall meant Pie Inspectors did not pull raids at certain yacht clubs.

But what brought an ex-sugar 'legger to Murkey's now?

Bunz watched a couple of Guys cast their fishing lines into the water, past the exposed riprap. He wondered what the heck they were hoping to catch, with the water so low and still ebbing. He looked across at Murkey's. Without the dreamy neon glow that it had at night, the diner was just an old waterfront shack in need of fresh paint.

The drivers of the shiny, late-model cars streaming toward the Golden Gate Bridge didn't give it a glance.

Don't know what they're missing. He started toward the old beauty. There was still too much to figure out, and until he did, Murkey's wasn't safe.

Bunz pushed open the door, hoping Webbs was already there. Climbing was a spider's game. *If he's not here, I guess I'll need a ladder and a good cup of coffee.*

19: Under the Diner

The swinging glass door closed behind him. Bunz looked around the diner. Disappointment! No spider. The afternoon waitress, Marge, waved her pencil.

"Hi, Bunz. Be right with you."

"Don't bother, Marge." Bunz walked behind the counter toward the kitchen door. As he passed the coffee pot, he grabbed a cup and sloshed some into it, taking a quick sip. "Who's in the back today?"

"The Bear, Lem."

Bunz saluted her with his cup and pushed into the kitchen. Behind him, the door rocked closed on its spring hinge. Fresh air blew in from the open back door, cooling the hot kitchen. The dishwasher was growling away. A jumble of dirty dishes waited their turn. Nothing cooking on the stove. Beyond the full pot sink, the kitchen crew was having lunch. They waved him over.

"Bunz! Come! 'ave zum lunch!" said Lem. "We fix for you zum'zing nice."

Munch, bright green alligator and builder of

sandwiches, pulled a stool over to the counter for him.

"Hey, Guys." Betting on their reaction, Bunz said, "Already ate. Down at Pier 40."

"What?" said Munch, her fork hanging in midair.

Lem shook his head and gazed at him sadly.

Bunz chuckled at their dismay. "Long story. What I do need is to pop open that hatch cover."

Lem looked at him, puzzled. "T'at old t'ing?"

"Won't be long," Bunz said. He set his coffee cup down and bent over the hatch. He hefted the handle. "Oof! Need a hand here."

"I'm done," Munch said, taking a last bite.

She stumped over on her short legs. Together she and Bunz heaved. The oil Ida had poured on the hinges last night had taken effect. The hatch cover opened smoothly. They swung it up and over onto the floor.

For the second time in less than a day, and with the same thrill of excitement, Bunz was looking through the hatchway. Many feet below where it had been last night, the water danced irregularly, slapping against the pilings. The low water revealed how tall the pilings were, and he could see that the water had been quite deep last night.

Still at least five or six feet deep now, enough for a small boat to navigate without grounding on the rocks.

Munch took a step back from the edge and peered through the opening. "Yow! I've always wondered about this thing. Why is it even here?"

"The old days," Bunz replied as he got down on his belly. "A smuggling leftover."

He inched forward and lowered his head into the opening. It was another world down there, dank and raw, a sharp contrast to the warm, bright kitchen. His long ears slipped through and swung in the breeze. He peered into the gloom.

With the tide down, the old stair was fully visible. He surveyed its rotted remains hanging from the underside of the kitchen—the old counter weights gone, the spring hinge long past working. Rusted metal stringers and a decomposed handrail were skeletons from the past. Twisting his neck, he could see the dark grey tips of the riprap close to shore, glazed with sea-growth and shiny from the lapping water. A short length of rusty chain briefly caught his eye. On all sides, the countless pilings crowded around to block his view.

He tightened his grasp and edged his torso further through the opening. Pilings blocked any line of sight. Whatever might be under here, it was not accessible from his insecure perch. He could see nothing of interest from where he was. His grip began to give out.

Nothing to see and too dark to see it. He felt a stab of irritation. *No spider when I need one.*

He pulled back and spun around, letting his feet dangle into the opening. "I've got to get down lower," he said to Munch.

He studied the stair relic. Rust had eaten away at the stringers. The wooden steps had long ago fallen into the bay. The lower part of the handrail fizzled out in midair, completely deteriorated. The whole contraption sagged toward the dark waters below. It looked none too stable.

Wonder if that thing will hold me.

Gripping the edge of the hatch, he stretched a trial foot down toward the stair, pressing some of his weight against the metal frame. Nothing happened.

So maybe not as lousy as it looks.

He tightened his hold on the hatch opening and shoved his foot hard against the old structure. It swung out from beneath his foot and let out a protest. *Schreee!*

Bunz pulled back. The stair groaned, and swayed back into place. Behind him, Lem jumped up.

"Vat you do, Bunz? We haf no accident here! Not on my vatch!"

Bunz waved a placating paw at Lem and scrutinized the stair more closely.

It's just for a quick look, he told himself.

He put his foot out again and pushed as hard as he could against the metal frame. *Schreee!* The stair swayed slowly out, then back again.

Bunz heard steps behind him. Lem stared down at him, mouth compressed, paws folded across his apron. Behind Lem, Munch's worried face fluttered.

"It's fine, Lem. Look!"

He stamped against the stair in quick rhythm. Despite the noise, the old steel did not give way. *Definitely not that bad*, Bunz thought.

He glanced back at Lem. "See? No reason to worry."

He turned his back on the bear, braced his paws against the hatch frame and eased down. His right foot he steadied against the stair stringer. Keeping a firm grip on the hatch frame, he bounced his entire weight against the stringer. *Schreee! Schreee!*

"Like I said, nothing a-tall to worry about!" He gave Lem a thumbs-up smile.

Lem shook his paw at Bunz. "You don't fall! Is not on menu today!" The bear stomped off.

Bunz grinned at Munch and took a deep breath. With his right foot solid against the stringer, he reached down and gripped the handrail with his right paw. With his left foot, he gingerly tested a remnant of wood tread. Seemed stable. He set his foot down and put some weight on it.

Snap! Without a wink, the wood splintered. His left foot was treading air. His left paw lost its grip on the hatch frame as his right paw skidded down the handrail. Both feet shot out from under him. Down he plunged.

"Aaaaa!" Munch yelped. She lunged to grab him, but too late.

His heart pounding, he flung his left paw at the handrail and clutched. There he was, suspended above the tide, both feet patting air.

Steady on, Bunz.

He cast an eye downward, searching for a place to set a foot. The narrow L-brackets would have to work! There was no other option.

He stretched out and wedged a foot into the corner of the nearest bracket. He pressed his weight down. The metal held. He jabbed his other foot toward the adjacent bracket. Pulling with both arms, he regained his balance and paused.

Well. Here I am. Might as well get a look. He peered around. There was no sweeping view of the underside of the pier.

Drat! Can't see the pier for the pilings. Just one more bracket down. Maybe two. He slid his grip down the handrail and tested the next bracket. It held.

OK. In business. Just one more.

He tried the next bracket, then the next. Four brackets later, he thought, *Now I'm cooking with gas.*

He swiveled his head around and looked up. The murky underside of the pier spread above him. The loose chain swung about, making s-loops in the breeze.

The only illumination was reflecting up from the choppy water. The pier decking rested on hulking beams, cut from the mammoth forests that had once covered the west coast. A thicket of pilings held up the pier, yet from his new vantage point, they still blocked the distance. He looked back through the hatchway. Munch's worried face leaned above him.

"Hey, Munch. Got a flashlight up there?"

"Yeah." She smiled. "Hold on!"

While he waited, Bunz listened to the waves collapse against the riprap. Just below where he clung to the stair, there was a constant chatter of water sloshing around the pilings.

Munch's head reappeared. She held a large flashlight. She tied a length of string around it and lying on the floor, she swung it toward him. He lunged hard. The stair reacted by swinging off in the opposite direction. The flashlight danced just beyond reach.

Schreee! The rabbit waltzed sickeningly

above the tide. Water swept beneath him. He closed his eyes. His stomach rolled over.

"Whoa, Nellie!" Munch cried out.

With a leisurely pace, the stair swayed back the way it had come. He held on tightly and waited while his racing heart slowed and his stomach flipped back into place. The nearby chain flipped back and forth. At the end of it, a broken link shone with a fresh glimmer.

Stair must have banged it.

"Come on, cowboy!" Munch smiled encouragingly, and gently swung the flashlight toward the rabbit again.

This time her aim was accurate. With one paw gripping the flimsy handrail, Bunz gingerly reached out and snagged the flashlight. He clicked it on. The beam was weak. It reflected off the shiny slime, but revealed little else; totally inadequate in the dungeon of pilings. What a letdown.

The long pier did project hundreds of feet into the bay. From where the rabbit clung to the stair, there was no way of telling what might be nestled in the dim ranks of pilings beyond, or even on the backsides of those he could see. Could he be looking for something that was farther out?

He doused the light and looked across at the culvert sticking through the concrete of The Embarcadero wall.

What if that culvert is what they were trying to get to? But G.G. said that Smilin' was using the flashlight to look up under the pier. Was the stair itself the target last night? The stair was useless, but Moose might not know that.

"Darn." The water sloshed below.

What I really need is a small boat! I could get under here, maybe find what they were looking for last night. Too bad it's Doc's day off today.

He let the flashlight swing loose.

Darn that Webbs. If he was here, he could easily climb all over and do a real search. Could he be at the Old Anchor? Guess I'll go check. Grab a Rabbit Hole while I'm at it, loosen up some brain cells.

20: Unexpected Finds

A faint breeze brushed past Webbs and Marilyn as they walked up the gently sloping culvert. It smelled of decaying crud laid down methodically by decades of water percolating through drains beneath the city. However, the two spiders barely noticed as they stepped over soggy trash and swung their light beams in search of a clue. In the roving beams, the metal corrugations looked like ribs of corduroy disappearing into darkness.

After ten minutes, they came to a spot where the corrugations stopped. It was an opening! A new tunnel branched off and sloped toward the south.

"Wow!" Marilyn said. "I've never really thought about it! There's a whole world of tunnels under here, for drainage and whatnot."

"It's the whatnot I'm interested in," said Webbs. He watched his flashlight beam peter out into the stygian distance. "You know, we didn't think this all the way through—should have brought a compass and paper to make a map, like Lewis and Clark."

Marilyn smiled. "Well, Lewis, we can come back another time and do that. I'm thinking this is more than a one-shot deal." She skimmed her flashlight beam over the wall. "You can see we're still under the tide line, so let's keep going. I don't think we'll find anything till we get to higher ground."

"You mean higher underground, don't you?" Webbs joked.

Moose stumped along as Bill led him deeper into the tunnels. His hooves slushed through sticky muck left behind by uncounted gallons of city discharge that had flowed through the tunnels over the decades. The instant he took a step, the ooze closed over the hoof print he had just made. Occasionally his antlers scraped against the corrugations. He could feel them getting coated with some disgusting mixture of weird scum. Half-rotted junk showed up in his flashlight beam. A shoe, tangles of sticks and mud, a sodden book. He stepped over it all and hustled to keep Bill in sight.

He had to breathe shallow so as not to choke on the noxious air. There was no way to know where he was, and Moose knew he could never retrace his steps. He very truly did not want to get lost in this dark and stinkin' maze. It all looked the same to him.

Sometimes he thought he saw the same junk he had already seen. Every now and then, he tried to ease his aching back by straightening up. But his antlers butted against the culvert every time and the nerve in his neck reminded him that it was a bad idea.

He kept a grim focus on Bill. His thoughts cycled around which method exactly he would employ to take care of Bill the Big Crumb Bum when all of this was over. No idea was too hideous.

And advancing ahead of Moose? Bill never hesitated. He knew the tunnels perfectly and had no trouble keeping up a pace difficult for the rattled Moose to follow. A turn here, a U-turn there—as though he had gotten confused and gone the wrong way. Sometimes they passed an opening and kept straight on. Sometimes they turned into it. Every so often, Bill heard a 'klong' and a string of profanity as Moose cracked his antlers into the culvert.

Bill smiled deviously. If they had gone straight to Murkey's, it would have taken thirty minutes, tops. But just to keep Moose baffled and in a cooperatin' mood, Bill had thrown in an extra twist here an' there. Bill hadn't lasted in business as long as he had by trusting his partners.

They'd been underground a solid hour.

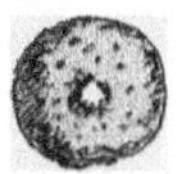

Bunz leaned against the scarred wood bar at the Old Anchor, sipping a Rabbit Hole—fresh carrot juice, gin, a squeeze of lemon. The history of the old bar was written in the hieroglyph of dents and dings that covered it. He watched the sun spread across them as he mulled over what Ida had just told him.

He watched as she poured a beer. "You say M'Boy asked about Towtruck?"

"Yes. Hamms said he was a dishwasher, years ago." Ida saw the rabbit brooding. "That mean something to you?"

"Sort of." Bunz paused while Ida delivered the beer. No need to trouble her, but Bunz knew it was Towtruck the dishwasher driving the night that truck crashed in front of Murkey's. If Moose was asking about Towtruck, then for sure he was up to no good. He added drily, "Guy ran with a flaky crowd. And I don't mean the bakers."

"Ha-ha. Well, I think there's a chance Moose is coming back to the diner tomorrow."

"Why is that?"

"I got Hamms to promise him blueberry pie tomorrow. Although after what you told me, I personally don't care to see him again." Ida glanced at the crowbar stored handy under the bar for unruly customers.

"I'll be there for blueberry pie!" Bunz said, sipping his drink. *Blueberry pie is not what the moose is after.*

He pushed his glass toward her for a refill and glanced toward the door, willing Webbs to walk in.

Where could that spider be?

"Think about it!" Webbs said.

He shone his light into another cross tunnel. "If some of these are the shanghai tunnels from the old sailing days, they'll run along the waterfront. There were places—you know, bars and rooming houses—where sailors were drugged and sold off to work on ships. Some of those places were likely turned into speaks, back in the day."

"Yeah," Marilyn said. "But let's save that explore for another trip. Right now, let's keep going straight. That way, at least we can't get lost."

"Good point. This one we're in heads west, toward downtown."

"That would be a good bet for bootleggers, too, don't you think?"

Marilyn half-listened as she inspected the walls where two culverts joined. "Look here, Webbs." Marilyn pointed with her flashlight beam. The bright light illuminated a seam in the metal. "There's a different material here, like this part going west was reinforced."

"Wow!" Webbs brushed off some dirt. "You're right. This stuff here is rusty, and the other metal isn't, like it's maybe aluminum." He looked further down the tunnel. "Huh!"

He gestured with his flashlight, making the beam waggle. A few yards ahead of them, a narrow wooden walkway had been built over the water trickle.

"Well, this is something!" Marilyn went over to it and stepped up. The walkway was slimy from years spent rotting underground. "Let's definitely keep going this way."

Their light beams bounced around the curved walls as the spiders hunted for breaks in the surface or markings that might indicate a hidden cache. Then, at the edge of the brightness, another gap appeared.

At first, it appeared to be just another branching tunnel but as they got closer, the darkness resolved into a doorway cut into the side of the culvert. There was another metal hatch, matching the one that had been installed at the mouth of the culvert. Set back and up a few inches from the walkway, it was attached to a wooden frame that was as solid as the day it had been built—with no gap at the bottom for spiders to slip under.

Marilyn and Webbs elbowed each other, too excited to speak for a moment.

Marilyn spoke first. "What do you think, Webbs?"

Webbs played his light over the door. No lock, but there were big steel dogs set on all four corners.

"I think we should try and open it," he said.

Suddenly, Marilyn flinched and darkened her flashlight beam. She stared past Webbs, westward down the tunnel. "Webbs!" she leaned over to whisper in his ear. "Turn off your light."

He darkened his light and turned to look the way she had pointed.

The two spiders stood still. Near and far, the echoing drip of a thousand water leaks shimmied more loudly in the inky dark. Nothing else stirred.

"I just saw a flash of light down there. Did you see it?"

"No. Was it maybe just a reflection of your flashlight off the water?"

Marilyn didn't answer. She kept checking down the tunnel. She was sure it had not been her flashlight.

"I don't see anything, Marilyn." The darkness was complete. "I mean nothing a-tall! It is freakin' dark in here!"

"Yeah. Maybe you're right. Perhaps it was nothing."

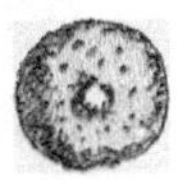

In a side tunnel, one hundred feet from the two spiders, Bill suddenly halted just a few steps from the tunnel junction. He doused his light and flagged Moose to stop.

"I heard voices," Bill hissed. "Turn out yer lousy light. An' quit clompin'."

As Moose halted behind him, Bill heard his partner's ragged breathing. *Do I got that Guy totally rattled or what. If he only knew.*

They listened in the dark. After a moment, voices floated to their ears. The sound was too faint for either moose to make sense of what they were hearing.

Bill slowly felt his way to the tunnel end and eased one eye around the corner. A couple of flashlights bobbed in the distance, too far for him to see who was holding them. Nearby, water dripped a steady measure of time and muffled the indistinct voices.

"That was a little freaky," said Marilyn.

"Yeah." Webbs turned back to the hatch and put his ear near to it, trying to block out the water's drippity-drip. He listened for a few moments. "I don't hear any sounds from the other side of this door. Let's see if we can open the dogs on this baby."

"OK." Marilyn shone her light on the door. "These dogs are as big as we are."

"But look," said Webbs. "You can see they used to keep the hinges greased up pretty good. Maybe we can still open it."

"Anyway, only the bottom two are dogged shut."

They set their flashlights down to shine on the door. Each spider wrapped a few legs around the handle of the dog and braced their other legs against the frame.

"OK. I pull, you push," said Webbs. "On three. One, two, three—Heave!"

The two spiders strained against the old hardware.

"OK. It moved a little, didn't it?" said Webbs. "Right. Again. One, two, three—Heave!" They grunted with effort. The handle moved a little more.

"We're getting it, Webbs! Let me get a better grip."

They kept at it, and slowly the dog moved free of the stop.

"Phew!" said Webbs. "Let's rest a minute, and then we'll get the other one."

They sat back and studied the other dog. "Doesn't look any worse than the one we just got," said Marilyn.

"I wish we'd brought water," said Webbs.

"Yeah. Didn't think of it," said Marilyn. "You ready?"

"Grrrrr!" he growled. "Let's do this!" Webbs flexed his muscles. "Jus' call me Ah-nold."

Marilyn smiled as she got her grip on the second dog. "Just call me ready," she shot back.

Webbs set himself and in his deepest voice said, "Vun! T'u! T'ree!" Together they shoved.

"Oof!" said Marilyn. "This one's a little stuck."

"Again!" said Webbs. They strained against the old metal. It didn't budge.

"Not happening," said Marilyn.

"OK." Webbs sat back. "Let's try this. Instead of big heaves, let's do quick hard jerks on it, one after another, OK? Boom-boom-boom. Just keep it up."

"Yeah. Ready?"

They grabbed the stubborn old dog and jerked it as hard as they could. Little by little, it moved. They doubled their efforts. Slowly it scraped back off the stop.

"Hey-hey!" crowed Webbs. "We got it!" He did a little dance of celebration.

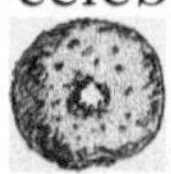

The two moose lurking in the cross tunnel quivered when they heard "We got it!" reverberate through the metal tube. The far-off flashlight beams flickered oddly on the walls.

Moose started to do a nervous shuffle with his hooves. Bill felt Moose's hot breath ruffle the fur on his neck. He moved away from the smell of it.

Gotta keep him quiet. Bill whispered a lie in Moose's ear.

"Listen, this ain't nothin'. There's stuff down here alla time. Sewer workers and like that."

He heard Moose gulp air.

Might a' got him too rattled, he realized. *Enough fooling around. Better git 'im straight ta Murkey's.*

He felt in his tool kit for his hammer. He wanted it handy, just in case Moose cracked.

Only one real problem: whoever was down here with them, they were in the way.

Webbs set his flashlight to shine at the door and said, "OK! Now to open the door."

They looked up at the heavy steel door looming over them. The hinges were on their side. They would have to pull it open.

"How 'bout this," Webbs proposed. "I climb up and push against that handle. You stay down here and pull against the bottom edge."

"OK," Marilyn agreed. She wedged a couple of legs between the door and the frame.

"Ready!" she said.

"OK. Pull!"

"Oof," said Marilyn. "Wait a sec." She reset a couple of her legs against the doorframe. "OK. Again!"

To their surprise, the door cracked open. Without a word, they increased their efforts. The old grease, applied years ago, did its job and without warning, the door picked up speed and swung wide open.

At once the spiders jumped off, sure that the door was going to carry them all the way around and smoosh them against the tunnel wall. But, as they watched, the heavy door slowed and stopped at the halfway point.

21: Caught

Webbs and Marilyn peered around the edge of the open hatch. There was only darkness beyond. A musty dry smell flowed from the inside, as old air crowded the opening and wafted into the tunnel.

Too excited to speak, they crawled up and over the door threshold and shone their flashlights into the darkness. Their lights skimmed around a long rectangular room. Dusty wooden tables and chairs were lined up against the long sides. Trash littered the floor, casting long flaring shadows in their moving lights. An empty wastebasket lay over on its side. Small pallets were lined up along the center of the room. From the high ceiling, light fixtures hung low. On the far wall, a second door led to somewhere else.

It was as though someone had shut the door one day and never returned.

"Outstanding!" Webbs said under his breath.

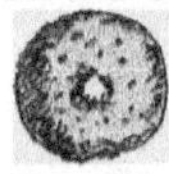

Flashlight off, Bill slo-o-wly inched into

the main branch of the tunnel, more silent than the still air. Moose crowded close behind him, so close that Bill could count the other moose's pounding heartbeats. Ahead of them, the two distant flashlight beams disappeared and the voices faded to a faint murmur.

The two moose eased forward, one deliberate step at a time. Bill wanted to sneak close enough to hear what these interlopers were saying.

Figure out what they're up to. Decide if they need to be taken care of.

Marilyn's eyes glowed. A secret room!

The two spiders walked over to the pallets. Four were empty. One held a couple of large, dusty sacks, stacked on top of each other. Marilyn leaned in to read the dust-covered label stamped on the bag. She turned to Webbs.

"It says Cement," said Marilyn, grinning.

"Cement? Like that newspaper story!" Webbs did a little jump and grinned, too.

Marilyn swung her flashlight low along the floor. The light beam lit up thick dust. And within the dust, tiny white particles glinted.

"Ah ha! Webbs. Doesn't this look like sugar to you?"

"Sure does."

He shone his light on the bags. Under a small tear, he held out a front leg. A few granules trickled out. "Mmmm! Tastes like it, too." He laughed. "So, we got sugar 'round here, we do!"

"I wonder where we are," said Marilyn, shining her light at the ceiling as if to see through it to count the number of floors above. The plain plaster ceiling and empty walls gave no clue.

Her light caught on an old-style push-button light switch next to the interior door.

"Hey! Do you suppose that old light switch works?" She walked over toward the door.

"Try it," said Webbs.

Webbs shined his light at the square wooden table leg while Marilyn climbed up. She laid her flashlight on the table, scurried over to the light switch, and reached up. With a little effort, she managed to push the button in. The room flooded with light.

She turned, smiling. "Ta-daa! Still works!"

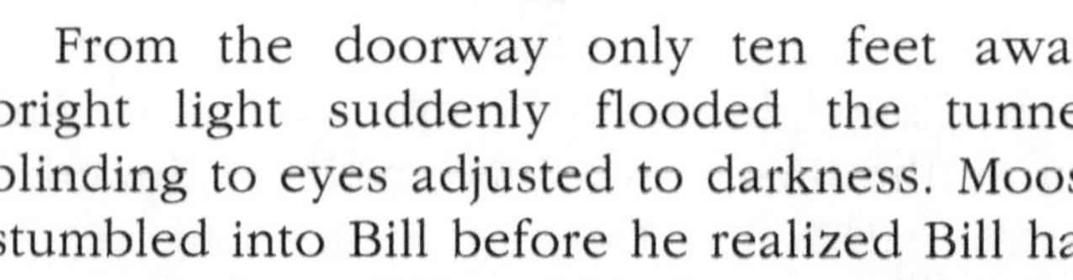

From the doorway only ten feet away, bright light suddenly flooded the tunnel, blinding to eyes adjusted to darkness. Moose stumbled into Bill before he realized Bill had stopped short. Bill wobbled. Moose clutched at Bill while they regained their footing.

"Sh-s-s-s-h," Bill hissed. His first impulse had been to run for cover, but he made himself stop and stand stock-still. Those two in the room didn't yet know they had company. Running would make noise.

As one moose, they both stepped sideways into the shadow behind the half-opened door and froze.

Marilyn flinched. "Hey," she whispered. "Did you just hear something? Out in the tunnel?"

"No." Webbs listened. "I don't hear anything. What did you hear?"

"It was like a clunk, or something."

They stayed quiet for a few moments, but heard only the sound of water. Webbs turned off his flashlight, set it on the floor, and climbed up to join Marilyn on the table.

"I guess it was nothing," Marilyn said, still whispering. "I'm more nervous than I realized."

"Maybe it came from upstairs in this building," Webbs suggested. He saw she was worried and added, "I think we're both a little on edge. But you have to admit," he gestured around the room, "this room is a fab-tabulous find!"

From the table top they surveyed their

discovery—a forgotten hideaway, full of stuff no one had seen in years. After a bit of self-congratulation, they toured the tabletops. Dust-covered equipment was spread across them: each table had two scales, packets of small bags, and pads of paper. Unfortunately, the walls were bare: no hidden compartments.

Marilyn brushed off the top sheet of a pad and studied it.

"Look here, Webbs," she said, her voice rising in excitement. "A form for listing how many small bags you fill, weight, date, name, time spent. And, here—this pad's an order form."

"Splitting up the sacks of sugar to sell on the street," Webbs said absently. His mind was wondering which way the little bags went after they were full. Back out through the tunnel or through the inner door? He walked over to the edge of the table and jiggled the door knob of the second door.

"Locked."

"I bought sugar on the street a few times," Marilyn said. "Crazy expensive, but I really couldn't stand that fake stuff."

"Yeah. Sometimes I bought sugar, too."

"It's hard to believe that preposterous mess we had to put up with that stupid Sugar Ban. Didn't solve anything, did it?" Marilyn continued. "You'd think they would have learned that lesson during the first Prohibition."

Webbs studied the door lock. "What building do you suppose this door leads to?"

"I would sure love to know. You're right about making a map," Marilyn said.

"Yeah," said Webbs. "It would really help to know where we are in the city."

For Webbs, the excitement of finding this secret room was fading. Even if this sugar den had been used by Murkey's, why would it matter these days? He didn't see anything here the moose might want.

Marilyn looked at her pal. He appeared a little down. How could that be? They were having such a great adventure. "What about these cement sacks, Webbs? How can they not tie back to the smuggling ring that operated that sugar truck in the accident?"

"It doesn't really matter. It's just sugar, now. Who cares?"

Marilyn was persuaded that this meant something. "That's our Murkey's connection!"

"Then what? Sugar doesn't matter like it used to."

Out in the tunnel, Moose had a sudden suspicion: *What if Bill had set him up?* The few words he caught from inside the bright room painted a disturbing picture. Words like 'we got it' and 'splitting up' filled his head.

So, that's why Bill cut himself into this deal and why these two other Guys is down in this ghastly tunnel. Bill called a couple pals and they think they're gonna bushwhack me as soon as I grab my stash. Moose snorted and coldly drew back a step. Bill elbowed him to keep quiet, for Pete's sake. The voices stopped, and then started again.

Bill turned to Moose and pointed down the tunnel as he whispered into Moose's ear.

"That way. Murkey's. We sneak past."

Moose hissed into Bill's ear. "I don't think so."

In the dim light behind the open hatch, Bill stared into Moose's glowering eyes. He did not like what he saw.

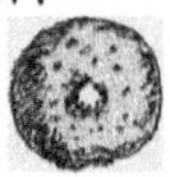

"You know what we should do?" Marilyn said. "Walk straight out, without stopping, and time how long it takes. Then we head in the same general direction on the streets and see where we end up. If we're anywhere near a Sprinkhels building, that's a possible connection!"

"That's a good idea," said Webbs, perking up at the thought of uncovering new information. "There's really not much to look at here. What say we head back out?"

Marilyn waited by the light switch as Webbs traversed down the table leg. Just for a joke, when he was halfway down, she switched off the lights. After the brightness of the ceiling lights, the sudden darkness was darker than ever.

"Whoa!" said Webbs. He stopped crawling. "Kinda dark in here."

"Yeah. A little too dark. Wait a sec."

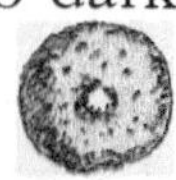

As Bill and Moose glared at each other, the light beaming through the hatchway went out. All was darkness.

Now! Moose thought. He blazed into action.

With a hard shove, he pitched Bill against the culvert wall and turned quickly. A flashlight flicked on inside the room. In the faint light, Moose saw instantly how the big door could be locked down—heavy metal dogs on all four corners. He grabbed the hatch door and rammed it shut. The tunnel went completely dark. Echoes clanged both ways down the culvert.

Steel scraped steel as Moose latched onto each dog and forced them all closed, as tightly as a big, angry moose could. And that was very tight.

Moose stood back. He flexed his shoulders. *That felt good.*

He switched on his flashlight and shined the light around the sealed hatch, checking each dog. Then he turned toward Bill.

Bill warily took a step back. *What the hay is going on in that bent brain of his?* Bill wondered. He felt around in his tool kit, and casual-like, slipped the hammer out and held it behind his back, at the ready.

Moose leaned in close to Bill and demanded, "How far now, Bill?"

Webbs panicked and clung to the table leg as the deafening clang filled the dusty room. Marilyn jerked in surprise and dropped her flashlight. It rolled to the table edge and smacked down onto the floor. With the sound of breaking glass, the room went black again.

Two spider hearts raced in panic. Horror-struck, they heard the dogs wrenched closed. All four dogs, all four corners of the hatch, sealed shut. Then, nothing. Several minutes went by. In the dark, Webbs turned toward Marilyn.

"Marilyn?" he whispered, without realizing it.

Marilyn replied quietly, "Webbs? You OK?"

"Yeah. Hold on. I'm just climbing down to the floor so I can feel around for my flashlight."

"Be careful of that broken glass from mine."

"Oh. Good point. Maybe you could reach that light switch again."

"I'm trying. Wait a sec. Ahh. Oops! Here we are." There was a click, and the room lit up once again. Marilyn peered over the edge of the table, down at her friend. "What *was* that?" she asked, still shaking, her eyes wide with worry.

"I don't know. Who the heck else would be down here?"

"Look at the hatch! All the dogs are tight shut."

Webbs didn't know what to say. He picked up a piece of crumpled paper from the floor and swept broken glass into little pile. "We'll figure something out."

"We'll never open them." She didn't add what they were both thinking: they were stuck, locked beneath the city and none of their friends knew where they were.

Holding his flashlight, Webbs walked over to the hatch and tried opening the nearest dog, but it was jammed so hard he knew they would never move it. Holding an ear near to the hatch, he listened. No sound. Marilyn watched him from the table.

"No one knows we're here, do they?"

Webbs had no reply to that. He wandered back toward Marilyn and swept an errant piece of glass into the little pile. He had a thought. "What about that other door? Maybe there's a crack under it."

He ran over. Marilyn followed him along the edge of the table. The crack beneath the door was narrow, too small even for Marilyn. He huddled on the floor and pretended he didn't want to cry about how stupid they had been not to tell anyone where they were going. They were sealed in. There was no way out. The only thing to eat was sugar and they had nothing to drink.

"Hey, Webbs. What's this?"

Marilyn was pointing to an ornate pipe attached to the wall next to the door. It started halfway up the wall and disappeared through the ceiling. The end was covered by a decorative hinged cap, held shut by a small spring.

"Oh, that," Webbs said. "It's a pneumatic tube, old-school for sending messages and small stuff. A suction was created that would suck a special cannister through the tube. This must be the basement of an old office building."

"I guess this was before fax machines, huh?" Marilyn joked, trying to get him to smile. "I wonder if the pneumatic still works." She crawled up the wall and hung from the cap. It didn't open. For some leverage, she braced herself against the wall and pushed. It remained closed.

"It's stuck," she said, swinging from one leg and waving the others in the air. She turned upside down in midair and smiled down at Webbs.

He smiled back. Even in a situation like this, his friend was still joking around. "Maybe the spring is just tight. Hold on." He crawled up beside Marilyn. Straining against the spring, they managed to open the cap a crack. There was no suction in the tube.

Marilyn and Webbs examine the old pneumatic tube.

"Do you suppose we could climb through here and get out at the other end?" she asked.

"It's worth a try," said Webbs. He aimed his flashlight up inside the tube. "We have nothing else. If there was suction, we could just get sucked up to the other end instantly." He smiled at the idea of pneumatic spiders as he examined the tube. He turned to her. "I'm not going to fit in here, but you will. You're going to have to go and bring back help."

"Oh." Marilyn swallowed a sudden lump in her throat. "OK. I can do that. But—" she paused. "What if whoever shut the hatch comes back?"

"Well. I guess we hope that doesn't happen." Webbs said it with as much sangfroid as he could manage. "I don't see any other way. Do you want to take my flashlight?"

She thought about it and shook her head no. "Too much to carry." She smiled a brave smile and said, "So then—I guess here I go!" Webbs held the cap open and she hefted herself into the tube.

"Be careful," he said. "When you get out, go straight to Murkey's."

"Will do! Fast as I can."

"Look for a rabbit with long ears. That's Bunz. Tell him what happened and you all can figure out what to do." He paused and added wryly, "You know where I'll be."

She smiled from the tube. "OK, Webbs. Count on me!"

And then, she was gone. Webbs let the cap snap shut.

"Now what," he said to the empty room.

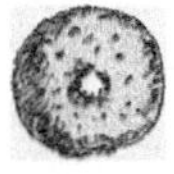

In the dim tunnel, Bill tried to decipher Moose's expression. "It's not far now," he said.

Moose shook his antlers. "Exactly how far?"

"Twenty minutes. Tops. Pro'lly less." Something in Moose had flipped. Getting him befuddled in the tunnels was no longer an edge.

The tone of Moose's voice threatened. "Get goin'."

"Yeah." Bill tugged his tool pouch. He was tired. Things were going sideways.

He limped off down the main culvert and set as fast a pace as his bum leg would allow. The slick wooden walkway creaked and cracked under the weight of two moose. In the slime, Bill's bad leg skidded. He wrenched his back and pain shot down his leg. But he didn't stop; he didn't speak.

He knew he would have to make his next play with Moose carefully.

And he was going to need a back-up plan.

"Another Rabbit Hole?" called Ida.

Bunz pushed his empty glass across the bar. "Just carrot juice this time." He heard the street door open. He swiveled around on his stool. No spider walked in. It was Doc. He waved the tiger over.

"I guess it's a 'good morning' to you, eh Doc?"

Doc nodded and slid onto a stool next to the rabbit. He watched as Ida put the glass of juice in front of Bunz. "Just carrot juice, right?" she asked.

"Yeah. For now."

Ida turned to Doc.

"Mornin' there, Doc. Get you an eye-opener?"

"Hi, Ida. Maybe a milk, if you have it."

"One milk for the cat!" Bunz called out, a smirk on his face. He turned to Doc and said, "So—what's up, Doc?"

Doc gave Bunz a chilled look. "How many of those things have you had that weren't 'just carrot juice'?"

Bunz smirked. "Aw-w-w, Doc. I got a tetchy tiger by the tail?"

Doc glowered at Bunz, rose up from his stool and slid over to the next stool.

"Aww, c'mon, Doc. Bring the cat his milk, Ida. He's not ready for prime time yet."

"I'm just wondering," the tiger growled, "do you know how G.G. got on this morning."

"I'd say pretty good: we found her boat!"

22: Marilyn to the Rescue

Marilyn's heart jumped as the cap snapped shut behind her. Inside the long metal tube, total darkness greeted her again. The confined space was even more silent than the sugar room had been.

OK, Marilyn. Buck up, spida'. What's the worst that can happen? Nothing. It's too narrow in here for anybody else to squeeze in. Even Webbs doesn't fit. Anyway, if something happens, you go back down to Webbs and— and what?

This tube is the only way out. So, let's go. I bet Queen Latifah is never scared. Chin up! Legs motivatin'!

Time to climb tough!

An unexpected whiff of fresh air cut through the stagnant funk of the tunnel to tease Moose's nose. He took a deep breath, the first since he had stepped into this ordeal a lifetime ago.

Smells like the bay, he thought. And just

like that, his stomach unclenched. Impulsively he straightened his back. Smack! His antlers cracked up against the top of the culvert. The nerve in his neck tweaked. *Ow! Doggone it!*

He cricked his neck sideways and smiled despite the neck pain. They really must be almost there. He picked up his hocks and trod after Bill. No telling which way that blunderbuss would turn next.

Abruptly, the clopping of Bill's hooves on the wooden walkway changed to clanging on metal. Moose hurried forward. A minute later, his light beam picked out the end of the walkway. Just ahead, past Bill, he saw a brightness that was not coming from Bill's flashlight. The end of the tunnel—it had to be!

Moose slowed his pace as he saw Bill halt in front of another old hatch. Pricks of bright light filtered in through the small holes perforating its surface, tiny laser beams filtering the darkness.

To Moose, the shimmer of the beams looked like heaven's stars.

With Marilyn gone, the sugar room suddenly seemed much more isolated. *What if she never came back? She could get stuck in the tube and be unable to get back down. What if she couldn't open the cap at the other end? What if?*

Webbs shook himself. He was in a mess. Panicking would not help. Besides, it was too late to lose his nerve. What to do while he waited?

Webbs went back to the tunnel hatch and surveyed the door. Flexing his muscles, he said in his best Austrian accent, "I am zee Terminata' Zpidah! I vill conkor zhis doarh wi' p-u-r-r-e Zpidah muscle!"

Gripping the nearest dog, he shoved with all his might.

"Ummmfphh!!"

Nothing. He changed his grip and pushed his hardest against the stubborn metal. "OOOF-Ummmfphh!!"

The dog did not budge. Not even a tiny bit. That punk in the tunnel had truly jammed it.

OK-OK, Spide. Time for Plan B. He sighed. *If only B. was here,* he thought morosely. *At least we could be stuck together. Ha-ha, 'stuck together.' B. would like that one,* he thought sadly.

Come on, Spide! Can't give up now! He strolled over to the other dog near the floor. He smiled the widest smile he could manage and bowed ceremoniously to the empty room.

"Ladies and Gentlemen! El Spidor will now astound and terrify the audience with his tremendous feat of Raw-w Power-r!"

He gripped the dog. He shoved. He heaved.

He shook his head.

Not gonna happen, Spidor, he said to himself. *Those dogs might as well be welded shut.*

He glared at the hatch for a few moments. *Who slammed the door and locked us in here anyway? Why?*

He turned back to the room. What next? At a minimum, he figured he was going to be stuck for an hour. Realistically, probably more.

Had even five minutes gone by? He looked around his cell and began to count.

First, he counted the tables: 8.

Then the chairs: 8.

On 7 of the tables was a scale.

9 boxes of small plastic bags.

10 order tablets.

4 orders-filled tablets.

2 pencils (one broken).

5 light fixtures.

5 wooden pallets.

2 sacks of old sugar marked 'Cement' (one bag with a hole).

1 wastebasket.

27 pieces of trash.

600 squares of linoleum on the floor.

1 light switch.

And 2 doors—both locked solidly.

No food, no water.

Just like a desert island, he thought. *But no palm trees.*

He wandered over to the sugar bags and ate a few sugar grains. Not so good when it wasn't baked into a donut. He did a few calisthenics. After that, he ran out of stuff to do. He picked up the one remaining good pencil and considered starting his memoirs on the back of an order form.

Marilyn felt like she had been climbing for a crazy long time, but she had no way to tell. She began to consider just how long the pipe might be. Fear crowded into her mind.

It's going to end eventually, she told herself. *I keep on till I get there. No second thoughts.*

But—suppose I get to the top and it's sealed shut? Suppose this, suppose that—fears launched themselves, one after the next, circling her mind, but she refused to let them stop her.

Climb, climb, climb. Up she went.

Then, without warning, the side of the pipe vanished as it curved away from under her feet. She patted carefully and followed as the pipe made a ninety degree turn, and there she was, on a horizontal surface. Was this the top? She rested for a few minutes and listened. Nothing but quiet.

Creeping slowly forward, she was stopped

with a jolt as her nose smushed up against a flat surface.

The end of the tube, she thought, as she bumped. *I found it!*

Her heart thumped. She heard a faint sound, maybe a voice. Her heart beat faster. What was on the other side? And more importantly, who was on the other side? The one and only way to find out was forward!

She felt around the edge of the cap to see if she could tell where the spring was that held it shut. It was completely smooth.

Dumb, dumb, dumb. Webbs beat his head against the floor. Caught up in the excitement of the moment, neither he nor Marilyn had thought to tell anyone where they were going. How foolish was that?

He thought back to the moment the hatch slammed shut. Had there been hoof steps—he thought so. One set, he was pretty sure—and then the massive door had swung shut with that deafening clang.

Must have been someone terribly big, to have heaved it closed so hard. Whoever it was must have seen the light in the room and heard us talking. So, we were locked in on purpose? It made no sense. What if that Guy wasn't alone? And what if they come back?

He appraised the room he had memorized by now. Where could he hide? Up by the ceiling? A lot of spiders liked it up high. But the ceiling was totally smooth and the light fixtures had no shades. They would see him up there and knock him down.

He could hide low, back under one of the tables—but they could too easily trap him. If he was found out, all they had to do was shut the hatch and there was no escape!

He meandered around the room, searching for some other place to hide, or something he could use to defend himself. Maybe they wouldn't shut the hatch right away and he could slip out before they saw him.

He paced the room. Sugar crunched under his feet. His glance fell on the dusty bags of sugar.

Ah-haaa! His eyes lit up with an idea. It might just work. *Time for a spider web!*

Marilyn leaned against the cap and thought, *Would this cap be more likely to open on the side, the top or the bottom? Hmmmm. I have no clue. No way to tell. Down where I got in, the spring was against the wall. But where is the wall up here? No way to know.*

She pushed stoutly against the bottom edge. The cap did not move. She shoved harder.

Nothing.

How will I even know if I just can't open it or if I'm pushing at the wrong spot? No way to know that, either. I'll just push my hardest and see what I see. So, the bottom isn't working. Right side next.

She set herself as best she could against the smooth interior of the pipe and pushed. Was that a waggle from the cap? She pushed against the right side a few times in a row. It WAS waggling!

So maybe the hinge is on the bottom and it opens from the top.

Excitement made her feel strong. She positioned herself upside down in the pipe and pushed. Light flashed into the darkness. Blinded by the glare, she flinched. The cap snapped shut.

She smiled in the dark. *Whew! Bright light! Wasn't ready for it,* she thought. *But I got it! OK. Again. Slowly, this time.*

She pushed against the cap once more and eased it open, just a little. As her eyes adjusted to the light, she listened.

There was a voice, audible but muffled, as though it came from an adjacent room. Closer at hand, she heard nothing. She pushed the cap open a little more and eased her head out to reconnoiter. The small room had tall open metal shelving along the walls, partially filled with boxes of office supplies.

Just a storeroom, she thought. *Good! No one's here.*

Pushing the cap open further, she held it with two legs. She maneuvered herself out and eased the cap silently closed.

Bill stood at the end of the culvert and examined the hatch blocking the entrance. Moose came up behind him and stopped.

"This is it," Bill said. His eyes looked the hatch over while his antlers probed for Moose's mood. "Comes out right below Murkey's. Here, hold my flash a sec."

Bill handed his light over to Moose and took a grip on the handle of the hatch. He pulled it toward himself then pushed it. He shook it back and forth with all his weight. It rattled, loose in the frame, but remained shut.

"Must still be a lock on the outside," Bill said. After a wary glance at Moose, he leaned down and sized up the wall holding the hatch in place. Rusty angle iron and rusty nuts and bolts attached it to the culvert. He selected an adjustable wrench from his tool belt. Fitting the wrench onto a large nut, he gave a big jerk. Nothing. He tried again.

Rusted tight as a tick's tail, he thought. He tried the remaining fittings. They were all just as bad.

Moose spoke up. "What about the hinges, Bill? Maybe we can pop these pins out."

Bill peered at the hinges. "Yeah," he growled. "Good thinkin'." He reached into his bag and put the wrench back. Out came a heavy screwdriver. He eased his hammer from his belt, where he had stowed it, handy-like.

"Shine that light here, 'bo." He wedged in the screwdriver and hammered against the bottom hinge pin. *Bam! Bam!*

The noise echoed down the metal culvert. He stopped.

"Hella noise."

They both listened. The sound of a boat motor passed. Water shushed against the shore outside. Above their heads, a truck rumbled down The Embarcadero. Car traffic swished by.

Bill said, "Pro'lly can't hear us."

He continued wedging out the hinge pins. In short order, all four pins were out, pinging onto the culvert as they fell.

The two moose stood for a moment and examined the deteriorating hatch. What was the next step?

Bill said, "How 'bout I pull on the handle; you push on the hinge side; we go back and forth, see if we can jimmy this thing open."

The two hefty moose took hold and shoved on the slab of steel. Back and forth, they muscled the hatch. Unceremoniously, it slipped off the unpinned hinges, lurched sideways, and swung straight toward them. They let go like lightning and quick-stepped backward, out of harm's way. The heavy steel stopped crookedly. It now hung at an angle, held upright by some unseen gizmo on the other side.

"So rusty it looks like a screen door," Moose said.

"Still plenty heavy!" Bill replied. "Come on."

Together they grabbed the unhinged side and pulled sharply. There was a loud "pop!" and the unseen gizmo gave way. Nothing held the hatch in place. The freed slab of steel lurched toward them.

Instantly and as one moose, they reversed course, pushing frantically against the toppling weight to stop it from falling on them. But it was too heavy. There was no way to stop it.

As it keeled toward them, the momentum drove them backward. At the last moment, they jumped clear and the slab cr-rashed onto the culvert, barely missing their quick-stepping hooves.

Creeping reluctantly away from the safety of the tube, Marilyn slipped behind a stack of paper and listened. In case she needed a quick getaway, she didn't want to be too far from the tube. There were so many places where spiders weren't welcome. She did not want to surprise someone and be squashed.

So far, so good. But where am I?

She eased along the back of the shelf toward the door. As she reached the shelf edge, a phone rang in the next room and someone picked it up. Peeking around the door frame, she saw a bare office and the back of a customer service parrot talking into a telephone headset.

"Thank you for calling. Your call is important to us. If you would like to hear this message again, press One. If you would like to hear a different message, press Two. If you would like to call again, please hang up and redial carefully."

Moose stepped onto the fallen hatch and said, "OK! Safe at the plate! No one hurt."

Bill sagged back against the side of the culvert, gasping. As he caught his breath, he studied Moose covertly. If Moose rushed him, he'd have to be ready. The hammer he had used on the hinge pins had fallen a few feet away. He glanced at it to gauge the distance, in case he had to grab it quick. But when he looked back toward his mistrustful associate,

Moose had turned away.

Fresh air swept into the culvert and Moose stood on the fallen hatch and filled his lungs. Nothing like a little excitement and fresh air to make a moose feel cheered. Bill leaned against the curve of the culvert, breathing heavy. Moose looked back up the culvert. No one lurked in the darkness. "Slick maneuver, Bill."

Bill slowly shook his antlers. "Gettin' too old for this fast life, man."

Moose looked down at the steel door. He wondered if Bill had been hoping to get him out of the way with a little accident. "Damn lucky no one broke a leg."

"So," said Bill, "yeah." He pushed himself away from the wall and took a step toward the hammer. "We made it, huh?" Moose made no reply. He stared across at Pier 13.

"There's Murkey's, just like I told ya." Bill eyed the back of Moose's head and took a step toward his hammer. One more sidestep and he quietly leaned down, picked it up, and slipped it into his belt.

"So, Moose. Where's this here stash?"

Marilyn crawled around the door jamb and scanned the office. A window, a parrot, a phone, a desk, and across the way, another door. Did it lead to the corridor or just to another office? Only one way to find out. She would have to sneak past the parrot.

The parrot was busy with another phone call. It was now or never. Marilyn darted across the office, squeezed under the gap at the bottom of the door. An empty corridor. An elevator! Down and out to the street!

Once on the street, she stopped to see where she was. North Beach! She had just come out of the big green copper building at Columbus Avenue and Kearny—one of Sprinkhels' buildings! Never mind that now! She was a spider on a rescue mission!

The late afternoon sun slanted across busy sidewalks. Keeping her eyes open and taking a couple of crazy risks, she scrambled over to Broadway and sped down the hill toward The Embarcadero and Murkey's.

Crossing the busy Embarcadero roadway was tricky. A thick stream of cars and trucks whizzed past. As she waited at the crosswalk, a wheelie cart rolled up. With a quick jump, she grabbed on and hitched a ride across to the other side. Back on sidewalk, she headed north, straight for Murkey's.

23: The Stash

With his back to Bill, Moose looked out of the culvert and smiled. It was a mean smile.

So. Ol' Bill wants ta know where the stash is. He's gonna find out, the moth-eaten, tick-infested double-crosser! And what'll it git 'im? Nuthin'!

The tide was down, the stony bay shore exposed. He could walk to Murkey's from here. He studied the riprap. An inch or two of water sloshed across the sharp stones.

"Wait here," he told Bill.

Slippery mud filled in between the stones. He'd have to cross a few yards of the treacherous stuff to get over to Murkey's pier. Tough going for a Guy with hooves.

Sure beats creepin' around them confound tunnels.

As Moose eased himself down from the culvert, his eye caught movement. He turned and looked further out the pier. A small boat! It bobbed about, tied alongside a ladder that led up to the rear of Murkey's.

Blood pounded in his head. *Was that the*

dog's skiff? No! Couldn't be!

He stared hard. He blinked and looked again. No. The dog's skiff had been white. He was sure of that. This skiff was blue. And it was too small.

Relax, Moose! Re-lax. That dog's a goner.

He took a moment to work out the cricks in his neck. Then he picked his way across the riprap. A hoof slipped and jammed into a crevice. *Steady there, Moosel ol' boy. Watch yer goin'. Can't slip up now.* He worked his hoof out and took a long, slow breath.

Final end o' the trail, Moose. What ya been waitin' fer. All them years in stir, and yer finally here. And yer money, tucked up high and dry, jes' like you was. Now here ya are, together again, ya lucky pup.

He looked up.

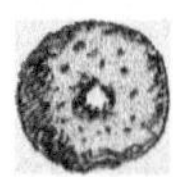

Out in front of Murkey's, the afternoon breeze ruffled Nosey's feathers as he poked around looking for snacks. He saw something move from the corner of his eye. Was it food, blowing down The Embarcadero? He turned.

No. Not food. Yuck. It was a fuzzy spider, and a little one, too, panting like a long-distance runner.

She ran right past Nosey and disappeared into Murkey's. A moment later, she rushed back out and dashed toward the curb, hopping up and down, inches from rush hour traffic.

Gonna get squashed if she tries to cross here. This ought to be fun.

As Nosey waited for his fun, Marilyn noticed the bird watching her. She veered over to him.

"I need your help!" she ordered. "Now!"

What's in it for me? he asked himself.

"There's trouble!" she said.

Not my problem.

She stomped a foot. "It's a real emergency!"

He watched her hop up and down. *Not tasty, but darn cute.*

Marilyn pierced the big bird with her fiercest librarian scowl. In a steely voice, she ordered, "Take me to the Old Anchor. Now! You're elected!"

Why not, he thought. *There's nothing going on here. They got tasty bar food at the Anchor.*

He leaned down. "Hop on!"

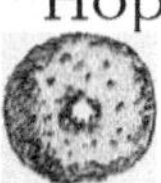

The Old Anchor was filling up with the after-work crowd.

"So," Doc said. "Your plan is to hang out in our kitchen 'til M'Boy shows up?"

Bunz nodded. "With the hatch open, I can see below and still cover the door."

"Great. Hamms will love a big hole in his kitchen."

"He'll listen to reason."

Doc looked doubtful.

"Gotta be ready for anything. If he comes by boat again, he'll see that stair is junk. To get into the diner, he'd use the front door."

Doc said, "He could use the pier access ladder I use every day. Come in the back door."

"Ladder?"

"Where I tie up my boat."

Bunz banged his empty glass on the bar. "Yes!"

"Another?" Ida called over.

"What?" Doc asked.

"Is your boat there now?"

"Of course."

"I need a boat, to get under that pier. You're elected!" Bunz headed for the door. "Come on!"

"Hold on, hotshot. Gotta finish my carrot juice thing here."

Moose leaned against one of the pilings that held the old diner above the tides. Noise from late afternoon Embarcadero traffic hummed in his ears. Out past where he stood, the old stair drooped in the air. He could see how little of it remained.

Good thing I didn't try nothing fancy at the

diner last night. My good luck's workin', Ma!

He waded into the bay and craned his neck to look directly above his head. His aimed his big flashlight beam around the pier's dark underside.

Long ways up. How 'm I gonna get up there?

Slowly he swept the beam back and forth, searching, probing. He played it carefully around the stair once more.

Slow down, Moose! Yer too excited. Ya missed it!

Anxiously he combed the area again. How could he miss it? He looked a fourth time.

Nope! Wasn't there!

He stiffened. His brain reeled. The beam flashed back and forth. Something should be there! And it wasn't!

A big beautiful barrel should be there! A waterproof barrel, chained absolutely under the diner. Stuffed with untraceable cash money snatched from the truck the night of the fake accident.

His light stabbed at the crusty old beams. His eyes raked back and forth. The broken chain hung down, teasing, useless, because his barrel was gone!

Gone!!

His Top-Secret Special-Order 100% Guaranteed Waterproof Barrel—gone! His Money! Stolen. His Brilliant Plan, his foolproof plan, the sweet dream he had held in his heart for Ten Long Years. Snuffed out!

Poof! His eyes went out of focus. Everything Ma had taught him about caution, about self-control, boiled away.

He stood up to his full height and let out a great roar! "Rrrrrrrrrrraaaaaaaaaaaaagghh!"

Bunz leaned against the bar and waited for Doc to pay his tab. He glanced toward the street door for the ten-hundredth time. Just as he did, a small spider rushed in. For a quick second, he saw a spider and spider meant Webbs! At last!

But then he realized, Wrong dad-blamed spider. Too small.

As he watched, she zeroed in on him and ran straight over.

"You're Bunz, right?"

The rabbit nodded.

"Oh, thank goodness!"

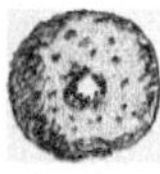

Moose shook with rage and kicked viciously at a piling.

No way did that barrel disappear by itself. It was Bill's stinkin' pals! Those Two Guys in the tunnel! They got here ahead of me and

*already snatched it. Well, well. They would
soon be pals on toast!*

From the opening of the culvert, Bill heard
the enormous roar. He observed Moose's
pantomime and sighed. Another bum plan
down the tubes. He tightened his grip on the
hammer, wishing he'd brought the big one.

Moose rushed across the slippery rocks
toward him. He was heedless this time of the
treacherous riprap. Bill watched, sure that
Moose would jam a hoof in a crevice and
go down. He was astonished when Moose
neared the culvert and picked up speed. In
an impossible feat, Moose leapt up, flying
straight at Bill.

Bill dodged sideways, but not fast enough.
Moose caught him in the shoulder, spun
the older moose aside and swept past. The
hammer banged down as Bill teetered at the
mouth of the culvert. He scrambled to keep
from crashing onto the rocks below.

"Better get lost!" Moose snarled. "Yer rotten
pals won't have my stash fer long and then
yer next!" Moose whirled around and stormed
off down the dark tunnel, flashlight beam
bouncing wildly off the curving walls.

Bill sagged. *My pals?* he wondered. *He
thinks I have pals?*

He snorted and slowly stood. He picked up
his wrench and screwdriver and stowed them

in the tool belt.

Shoulda put that Guy in the wacko wing at the Moosegow and thrown away the key. He's loony. Likely never was a stash.

But just in case, he retrieved his hammer and flashlight and limped down the tunnel after Moose.

"You crazy idiots!" Bunz fumed. He shook his head. His eyes betrayed his worry. "And he's still in there? You have no idea who shut you in?"

"Yes. No."

"Well, let's go! Ain't no one gonna mess with my spider!"

Ida hurried over from the other end of the bar. "Trouble?"

"What else?" Bunz said harshly.

Marilyn spoke up. "We'll need something to break that padlock. Webbs and I squeezed under, but you Guys won't fit."

Reaching under the bar, Ida said, "How about a crowbar?"

It clanked as she pushed it across the bar. Bunz grabbed it and they headed for the door. Bongo was just entering. The little dog saw the crowbar and whistled.

"What's up, Bunz?"

Bunz kept moving. "Tell you on the way.

Come on!"

They all swarmed the door.

Ida called, "Wait! Flashlight!" Bongo turned. She tossed it toward him. He snagged it mid-air and hustled after the others.

24: Ready or Not

Webbs had completed his arrangements. Spider-web trip wire? Check. Web sack in position above the hatch? Check. Clear path for trip wire between light switch and web sac? Check. Memorize exit path to the hatch? Check.

He counted steps as he ran his escape route one more time: from light switch, down table leg, along baseboard to tunnel hatch—he could easily be running it in the dark. In fact, he rather hoped he would be. When that clown came back, with luck and speed he would be out the open hatch to freedom!

Back at his light switch lookout, he sat down to wait. Time passed slowly. So slowly. How long had it been since Marilyn left? Twenty minutes? Two hours? The song that Ritchie Havens used to sing ran through his head: "Free-dom, Free-dom! Free-dom, Free-dom!" How long before that big Guy came back looking for him?

Much too soon, he had his answer.

He heard a distant thudding, muffled by the

closed hatch. It got louder. He recognized it. Hard-driving hooves pounding toward him on the wooden walkway. The racket intensified, and then stopped, right outside the hatch.

This is it! Just let that buster come on in. I'm ready.

From the other side of the hatch, he heard angry muttering. He reached up and punched out the lights.

Give my eyes a little time to adjust to the dark again.

There was a grunt beyond the door as the first dog scraped back.

Must be that same crank. Sounds plenty big.

One dog, then two. Webbs counted. Metal scraped against metal as he heard the third dog move. Only one more to go. The fourth dog was wrenched back. As though it weighed nothing, the hatch was heaved open wildly. It swung all the way back and banged hard against the tunnel wall. As the sound retreated down the culvert, Webbs heard snorting and heavy breathing. A flashlight beam glowed past the hatch frame and brightened the dark room.

"I know yer in here," growled a deep voice. "Y'ain't hidin' from me in no dark hole!"

Webbs gripped his trip wire. His heart banged in his chest. *Just step through that door, buddy boy. Nice and easy.*

"I know ya stole it, ya gol' durn sons a' tannin! Ya think ya can hide from Moose? Hah! Think agin!"

Moose? Webbs' mouth dropped. The moose named in the newspaper story?

Another loud snort. A massive figure stood in the opening, illuminated faintly by the reflections from the flashlight beam he swept back and forth around the room.

"Come on out, ya lily-livered toad-eaters!"

Webbs tensed. *Just a little further in, bud.*

Moose stepped up and filled the doorway. Right into the spider's target spot.

Now!

Webbs gave his trip wire a decisive jerk.

"Ahhhrrrrggg!" The flashlight dropped to the floor. Glass shattered, the light went out and the sugar den was all darkness once again.

The room filled with a stream of bad language, accented by hooves clomping. Instantly, Webbs jumped down from the table. No time for climbing! He felt his way past the table legs and moved along the baseboard toward the open tunnel hatch. Freedom was going to be his!

Suddenly, a new flashlight appeared at the hatch. A new voice filled the room. Webbs froze. The new voice sounded dry and a little irritated.

"What the hay is going on in here?"

"Dammit, Bill! Somethin' in my eyes, like sand or somethin'."

"Well quit yer stompin' around, fer Pete sake. Here, siddown. I got water."

A chair scraped along the floor. Webbs took a slow inch toward the hatch.

"Mother a' moose! Siddown, will ya!"

More moaning. The chair creaked as Moose sat down.

"Wait a sec," growled the second voice.

The flashlight moved across the room toward the second door.

Oh, no! He's headed for the light switch!

Not close enough to the tunnel door to make a run for it, the spider reversed course. He turned so fast, his hat flew off as he sprinted behind the nearest table leg.

Just as the lights flicked back on, he ducked into a corner of safety. He winked his eyes in the sudden brightness and looked back at his hat, marooned in plain sight. It seemed to glow in the bright light.

The seated moose moaned. Webbs peered from behind the table leg. Did he see two moose? Could they be the same two moose Ida had described? Hadn't she had said one of them was a short moose? These two were large and larger.

The moose by the light switch flicked off his flashlight and set it on the nearest table.

Must be the one called Bill.

Moose snuffled and moaned again. Bill limped over to the seated moose and unhooked a water bottle from his tool belt.

"Now be quiet and set still, will ya!"

The seated moose looked younger than Bill. Not so moth-eaten. He had his head down and tears flooded his eyes and dripped onto the linoleum tiles. He groaned.

"Tip yer fool head back," Bill told him.

Longingly Webbs eyed the water as it spilled across the seated moose's eyes and onto the floor. Wow, was he thirsty!

"Don't rub 'em. Jus' set there and blink! There. That any better?" Bill chuckled and took a swig of water. "Ya ain't the first Guy got sugar in his eyes, Moose. You'll live."

Jeez. A moose called Moose. That's silly. But he doesn't look silly. Just very enormous.

"The right one's still bad, Bill."

Bill poured a slow stream into the right eye. "How's that?"

"Awright. That's better."

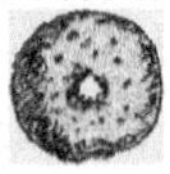

Nosey alighted on the lip of the culvert. Across the water, at Pier 13, Doc worked the oars to steady his boat at the foot of the access ladder. A tidal current schemed to push the little boat away as Guys swarmed down the ladder and crowded aboard—the rabbit, Bongo, the little spider, an alligator, and a crowbar. A full boatload!

Doc turned the boat and headed across the few yards to the culvert. It was heavy going with such a load. He put his head down and pulled hard. From the bay, he heard a boat motor approach. He looked up. A fishboat! It nosed in toward them.

What's a fish boat doing in here? he asked himself.

He peered into the wheelhouse. At the wheel was a big white dog—G.G.!

"G.G.!" Doc yelled.

Bunz turned. "It's the *Sea Dog*!" he shouted. He waved vigorously at G.G. to join them.

From the bow of the *Sea Dog* an anchor splashed down. An inflatable raft was tossed into the water. The big dog and a jaunty reindeer dropped down into it.

As Doc's little boat reached the culvert, G.G. and Finn rowed up behind them. There was a scramble from the boats. Marilyn scooted up the wall to the culvert.

"Good heavens!" she cried. "The hatch is busted open! Someone's been here!"

"What's all the excitement?" asked G.G.

"Finn! You and Nosey keep watch out here!" Bunz shouted as he plunged into the tunnel. "G.G., come on! Let's hurry!"

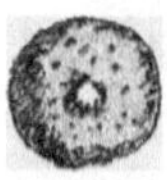

"Well, Moose." Bill looked around the dusty room. "Where are these so-called pals o' mine? I don't see nobody."

Bill hobbled across the room to the inner door. His limp was worse than usual—his bum leg was tired and aching, and his back was sore. He twisted the door handle back and forth.

"Locked. They didn't get out thataway."

Webbs squeezed himself into the deepest shadow behind the table leg and closed his eyes. Hooves clomped around the room.

Bill peered here and there and smiled to himself. He remembered this room and recalled other times—times when things were perfect for Guys with his proclivities and talents.

From the other side of the room he contemplated Moose. "So where are they, Moose?"

"They slipped out when I couldn't see and got away. Ain't it funny how you show up right after."

Loony as two full moons. Bill considered Moose's dripping face and made a show of shaking his head no. Moose's voice got loud. Bill listened silently as the outraged Moose went on with his loopy inventions.

"Yer pals stole what's mine, Bill."

Bill shook his antlers. "My pals?" he asked flatly.

"Yeah! Ya let 'em slip out right past me, then ya turned on th' light," said Moose. "I'll bet ya a golden goose yer gonna leave here and meet up fer the split!"

"The split." Bill leaned against a table to ease his leg pain. He sighed. *Where did Moose get his crazy ideas?* "Nobody slipped past me. And ya might recall, I ain't been outta yer sight since ya sold me on this pipe dream. So tell me, how'd they know we was comin' here?"

Moose got sullen. "Nobody sets me up, Bill." He leaned over and picked up his flashlight off the floor. "Nobody!" He flicked the switch. "Busted. Dang it!" He threw it back down, got up and grabbed Bill's off the table.

"Ya think I set ya up?" Bill was angry. "Do ya, Moose? Huh?"

"Why else would anybody be down in this god-fersaken hole? Ya heard 'em in here, same as I did!"

With the beam of light, Moose began to probe every inch of the room. "Where are they then? If they didn't slip out, where are they? And where's my money?" he mumbled.

He got to the tunnel door and shone the light around the rough door frame. Above the door, he saw a little sack drooping upside-down.

"What's this?" He poked it down with a pencil and peered at it. "Spider web. Sugar."

He turned to Bill. "Here's how that sugar got in my eyes, Bill. The little stone rats made a booby trap. And look—this thread goes al-l-l the way over to th' light switch. Wadda ya think, Bill? I think we got us a sneaky spider." He scanned the room. "Hidin' someplace."

As the big moose stepped out of Webbs' view, his hoof kicked at refuse on the floor. Something rolled toward the spider. Webbs groaned silently.

Oh no. My hat. He risked a quick peek. Moose was studying the ceiling.

Bill said, "Ya got something there, Moose." And Webbs heard Bill begin to limp around the room, searching inch by inch.

"Spiders usually like it up high." Moose chuckled ominously. "That way ya cain't step on 'em."

Webbs cringed. He flashed another stealth glance. He saw the two moose tag-teaming each other, slowly examining the entire room.

"Hey!" Moose flipped open the end cap on the pneumatic tube and let it snap shut. "Will ya look at this!" he said. He flipped the cap open and let it click shut again.

Bill leaned in. "Ya suppose they climbed out thataway?"

Now or never! Webbs took a deep breath and scrambled for the door!

From the corner of his eye, Bill saw movement. He turned.

"Ho! There goes one of 'em!"

Moose whirled and was after Webbs in an instant. The floor shook under the weight of the pursuing Moose.

"Git 'im. Moose, git 'im!" Bill yelled.

The spider fled just as fast as he could. Was he fast enough? The dark hatchway gaped maddeningly close. He gasped for air.

Almost there, Webbs! Almost there!

Hooves snapped furiously behind him.

More speed, Spide, more speed!

Then suddenly, bursting from the tunnel, a swarm of Guys exploded into the room! With shouting! And crowbars swinging! With falling moose and fur flying!

Spinning blindly, Moose crashed into the wall, hard and sudden. Felled by a wallop from the crowbar, he rebounded off the wall and tumbled to the floor. Bunz pitched a blow directly at his jaw. Moose howled in fury and tried to scramble to his feet. The rabbit leaped onto his tender nose and pounded away at it.

"Aowww!" yelled Moose. A hard little fist jabbed his eye. He swatted at the rabbit. Then it felt like the whole wall crushed down on his chest. He squinted with his good eye. It was that big white dog. She was not a dead dog!

She growled in his face and displayed a mouth packed with serious teeth. Her sharp claws dug into his neck. Dog breath flooded his nose. Pinned down, Moose struggled to shove G.G. off. He groped for something to strike back with. Stretching out a hoof, he grabbed at a nearby chair. Then, inches from his ear, he heard a new growl as sharp teeth bit into the tender ear. Another darn dog!

Across the room, Bill watched in dismay. He saw Moose go down and caught a glimpse of long rabbit ears.

That rotten rabbit! I knew he was trouble! The old moose put his head down and charged directly toward the hatchway.

Doc scooped up the crowbar and swung at Bill as he rushed past, landing a sharp blow on his bum leg. Bill howled and kicked out. Hopping forward, he found himself covered in a tangle of dangling spider web. And heading straight for him was a bright green alligator. She came in low and mean, took a big chomp on his hock and stayed there. Pain shot up his leg as he sidestepped a tiger and hoofed it through the hatch.

Bill hadn't moved that fast in years. He executed a smart turn to the right and took off down the tunnel to the safety of darkness, as fast as his gimpy leg and anchored alligator would let him.

Moose clutched wildly for some sort of weapon. Anything! A rhythmic thunder shook the floor. He turned his head. Inches away, a tiger slammed a large crowbar against the floor, right beside his head.

"Hi," Doc said, showing all his pointed teeth. Moose sighed and closed his eyes.

Up on a table, Marilyn danced with excitement. She had never seen such a big fight before.

Bunz paused, breathing hard from his recent exertion. The Guys had Moose M'Boy under control. The other moose had run off.

He looked around. Where was Webbs? Under a table, covered with dust, he saw a straw hat.

"Webbs!" he cried out. "Webbs, where are you?"

"I'm here, Bunz." The spider's voice cracked with tension. "I'm OK."

The spider stepped from behind the table leg.

The rabbit gave his pal a big hug. "You crazy galoot." No way would this spider ever get hurt, not one black fuzzy hair of his head.

"Thought I was done for, Bunz." Bunz shook his head as Webbs looked into his pal's eyes. "They were gonna flatten me—spider pancake! You got here just in time!"

From his position guarding Moose, Bongo said, "Where's that alligator?"

Just then, Munch limped back from the tunnel.

"He shook me off," she said. "Plus," she made a face and stuck out her tongue, "he tasted awfully gamey. Eecch!"

Bunz smiled at Munch and said, "Never mind. I know where he lives."

From up on the table Marilyn asked, "Who was that other moose?"

Webbs smiled up at his rescuer. "Some kind of partner. This one here," he looked at Moose, under guard on the floor, "he's the moose in that newspaper story."

Newspaper story? Bunz looked back and forth between the two spiders. What had these two been up to?

But what he said was, "So, Webbs—where's your hat?"

25: The Wrap Up

It was late in the night, or you could even say early the next day, after the fight. It wasn't a clear night. But not so foggy either. Not like the night before. Lights across the Bay Bridge formed a nebulous halo. From the window at Murkey's, a warm glow radiated out and lit up the sidewalk.

If you had stopped in for a bite, you would have seen a big, boisterous crowd of Guys sitting at the counter. After all the excitement, after the cops carted Moose M'Boy off once again, and after everybody got a ride in G.G.'s boat and helped her tie up at her home berth, Bunz and Webbs and all the Guys converged on Murkey's.

Ida cleared away empty plates. She shook her head and smiled to herself. What a story they told. What a fight! What a great bunch of Guys!

She pushed back into the kitchen with a load of dishes. Hamms was dropping donuts into hot oil. He called over to her, "So. Maybe now story time is over and you have time to help, eh?"

"I do!" She put the dishes down in a clatter and hustled over.

Out front, Finn was leading cheers for the tunnel warriors. Marilyn and Webbs had caught each other up on their adventures. Now, along with Bunz, they were trying to piece together the puzzle of Murkey's and Moose M'Boy.

Bunz listened while they talked. He was getting drowsy despite two cups of Murkey's great coffee. He hadn't had a good night's sleep since the adventure started.

"Moose was in town to retrieve a stash he had hidden. I heard him ranting at Bill about it," Webbs said. "He was convinced we had gotten to it first, and that we were in cahoots with Bill."

Marilyn said, "So he's got something valuable hidden somewhere."

"Not in the sugar room," said Webbs.

"Where could it be?" Marilyn mused.

"Maybe we search the tunnels again?" asked Webbs.

Bunz swiveled around on his stool and stared at the spider. "Haven't you had enough tunnels?"

"Just to be sure we didn't miss something," said Webbs.

"But that hatch was broken open from the inside. The hinge pins were out. Those two came through the tunnels, to get to Murkey's," said Marilyn. "The tunnels were the means to get here."

"Bunz looked under the diner and found nothing," said Webbs.

"Tomorrow we go under there and do a thorough search," said Bunz. "You're the climber Webbs, and we'll borrow Doc's boat."

"How do we look for something when we don't know what it is?" Marilyn asked.

Webbs' eyes gleamed. "I think know." He exchanged a glance with Bunz. "It had to be something he could get off that truck in a hurry—and sugar's too heavy. And he was yelling at Bill about 'the split'."

Bunz chuckled. Webbs was one smart spider. "Money, wasn't it," he said.

"You figured it out, too?"

"Bootleggers have to move two things," Bunz said. "Their product and their proceeds."

Marilyn sat back and smiled. "Of course! That truck was carrying sugar and sugar money!"

Webbs said, "Maybe Moose stole those sacks of sugar to distract from his real theft."

"I doubt he was too worried about cops," Bunz said. "A lot of them were paid off. I bet he was more worried about the Guy whose sugar money he stole. Unlaundered money—it's unreportable!"

"So where is the money then? We still should do a search," Webbs said.

"When I was under here yesterday, a piece of rusty chain was hanging down," said Bunz. "The end link was broken. And it was bright and shiny."

"So maybe he chained the stash under here and just recently it disappeared?" Webbs speculated.

G.G. walked over to listen in. "Could be it was still here last night, when Smilin' and I were under the pier."

"Well, that's a definite maybe," said Bunz. "Remember that deadhead banging around?"

"Yeah," Webbs nodded. "It could have knocked something loose."

"So," G.G. mused, "just imagine what might have happened if we had found that stash last night?"

"Probably nothing good. Anyway," Bunz smiled, "I think it's gone now. Murkey's is safe and that's the main thing!"

At this, a big cheer went up.

Just then, Ida pushed through the kitchen door. Doc and Hamms were right behind her.

"What's all the noise out here?" Hamms looked around mock-sternly. Ida held up a big tray of fresh donuts, all beautifully frosted. The Guys caught sight of the fancy donuts and cheered again.

Ida proudly set them on the counter, and asked, "Who wants fresh coffee?"

THE END

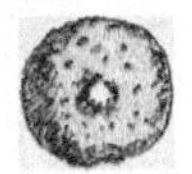

...or is it?

Out to sea, Joe and Pops Maartuni were having a good fishing trip. The fish were plentiful; the weather had cleared. An almost full moon shone a path across the dark waters. Pops was at the helm, enjoying the moonlight sparkling off the tops of waves. He scanned the horizon and checked the radar. No boats out here but his. He loved the freedom of being alone at sea in the night.

His practiced eye scanned the waters, always on the lookout for any unexpected flotsam or an unlit boat sneaking around. He'd been around for the Sugar Ban. He knew what smugglers could do! He hummed an old sea ditty and tried to recall the words. His eye stopped on something floating off his starboard bow, clearly outlined in the moonlight. It was a large wooden barrel, bobbing along with the ocean currents.

Pops said, "Tut-tut," and turned the wheel to steer his boat toward the sea-going debris.

"Joe," he called out to his son. "Joe! Come

up here and snag this thing, floating around all alone it is, such a danger to navigation!"

The barrel, floating in the moonlight.

About the Author

Lou grew up on a small farm in the foothills of the Berkshire Mountains, and has lived on both coasts of the United States. This has allowed many enjoyable car trips back and forth across this country. These days, when not creating Bunzini's world, Lou works as a deckhand on the ferries of the beautiful, ever-changing San Francisco Bay.

Lou discovered her first love at The Hickory Stick Bookshop, which is still doing business in her hometown, Washington Depot, CT. It was love at first sight. Her name: *Cinderella*. What was the first book you fell in love with?

Lou followed her mother 'round and 'round the store. She promised so hard that she would learn how to read, if only she could please, please take *Cinderella* home.

Her plan worked. She still has that book, although the cover somehow came off at the hands of a younger brother or sister. In her hometown, the most beautiful building was the Gunn Memorial Library. She loved to browse the old wooden shelves to discover the many unread treasures, checking out big stacks from Mrs. Hoadley, the librarian. When Lou is not writing, she loves nothing more than settling down for a good read.

Lou recommends other books she loves at: loucook.com

Author's Note

I would like to thank the key people who were invaluable in getting this book project to completion.

First is Don Malcolm (Bub), who instigated the world of The Rabbit just before Easter, 1996, at a Santa Monica, CA. drugstore. He purchased three plush Rabbits, with the idea of getting a silly laugh. Little did he know, but that Force of Nature we now call 'The Rabbit' began that day.

Next, I wish to thank Arthur Tashiro, the perfect editor, mental health adviser and overall consultant on everything. He is also my dear husband, a thoughtful man of many skills. Most importantly, he knows when I'm being funny and laughs at my jokes.

Third, my thanks to E.A. Sawabini for his wonderful drawings. He has known the Rabbit and all the Guys for many years, and with little input from me, understood what was needed to beautifully illustrate the Rabbit's noirish world.

Of course, finishing this book took much

longer than initially estimated. Isn't it always like that? There are those who gave up on my ever wrapping it up, so I particularly wish to thank the good-hearted people in my life who, over the years, took time to enquire how the project was coming along, and encouraged me toward the end game. You are rare and gracious birds indeed, and deeply appreciated.

In particular, I wish to mention J.P. Harrison. Her experience from a lifetime of artistic invention and her advice on many matters, large and small (and possibly the fact that we have been friends since high school), loom large in the history of writing this book. She blessed me with her conviction that my instincts could be trusted.

As well, I wish to thank Bonnie Britt. In addition to proof reading, she provided invaluable advice for a first-time self-publisher like myself. And she introduced me to Linda Dunn, virtual author's assistant. Without Linda, I would have gone insane trying to navigate all the requirements of a book launch and the social media world.

At no time in the writing of this story were any toys or animals, stuffed, living or dead, harmed in any way. Any mistakes or problems herein are solely mine.

What Is a Guy, you ask, and why is 'Guy' even spelled with a capital 'G'?

The curious can go to: bunzini.com and click on the page: 'What Is A Guy?' and read all about it!
ENJOY!

Connect with Us

Lou Cook Tweets: @Lou4Cook
And she is on FACEBOOK: Lou Cook, author
Bunz is on FACEBOOK as Mr. Bunzini
Look for **bunziniempire** on INSTAGRAM

Our **WEBSITES**:
More about Lou: **loucook.com**
Sign up for FREE fun and information with our Newsletter at **loucook.com**!
And find the Guys at: **bunzini.com**

References and History

Some of the history in this story was invented. Some is real history.

For those interested in the real history, explore these following fun, information-packed websites:

+ **burritojustice.com** This site has a lot of great links, as well.

+ **FoundSF.com** This site has a fun map: Tidelands-Auction-Map. You can see the changes in the shoreline of the bay over time as it was filled in.

+ **ShapingSF.org**

+ **The San Francisco Public Library** has many historical photos on line.

BOOKS

These books are also recommended. They can probably be found at a used book website, which is where I found them:

+ *Vanished Waters* by Nancy Olmstead

This book is about the destruction of Mission Bay. With many great photos.

My friend Rocky remembered Nancy talking

about her work on the book at the Eagle Cafe. The Eagle Cafe used to be located where there is now a big, ugly parking lot across the street from Pier 39. The Eagle Café relocated to Pier 39 as a result of the parking lot construction There is an historic photo with Rocky in it, up on their walls.

Rocky's recollections of the Eagle Cafe were my model for the Old Anchor.

+ *Recollections of a Tule Sailor* by Captain John Leale. Rocky leant me his copy of this book.

Captain Leale sailed into Mission Bay as a boy, while it was still a bay. He says it was the most beautiful place he had ever seen. He spent his life sailing the San Francisco Bay waters and its tributaries. After he retired, he wrote this wonderful book.

It is filled with first person information and his recollections of the early development of San Francisco. He sailed all over the bay as well as up and down many of its tributaries. He went to places that are no longer accessible by anything but the smallest boat, because the destruction from the Gold Rush filled the entire bay system with tons and tons of dirt washed down from the Sierra Mountains.

The book is so unique, I got a copy for myself.